# SNAKE EYES

Z. A. JONS

DreamPunk Press

Snake Eyes

by Z. A. Jons





Published by DreamPunk Press

ISBN 978-1-954214-92-7 (Garamond font)
978-1-954214-93-4 (OpenDyslexic font)
978-1-954214-94-1 (ePub)

# Contents

# 1

## NOT IN THE BEGINNING

"**M**s. Manley!"

Mel spins around, wobbly on the new left leg, fury in the fists held tight to her sides lest she take a swing at the nurse. She's already been cited twice for taking swings; she doesn't need another. Third time and all that.

"Staff Sergeant Manley. It's Staff Sergeant here!" *Here* is the VA counseling center in Bethesda.

"Fine. *Staff Sergeant* Manley. Get back inside." The male nurse is brawny enough to be a Marine and may have been one in a former life; his biceps strain the tight blue sleeves of his cotton tunic, making him look like the Hulk preparing to burst his seams.

Of course, if he'd been a Marine, he'd have called her Staff Sergeant from the beginning.

"No." Mel spins back around, hop-marching toward the little black Miata parked in the shade of a breezy elm in the end parking. Or trying to, anyway.

Her step hitches; she's not as sure as she should be on the prosthetic. The black ballerina flat on the right foot is scuffed on the toes, an unintentional casualty of her stilted gait. Its mate wouldn't fit on the foot part of the new prosthetic, so it was tucked into the top of her oversized purse.

Wearing her shoes had been one of the problems with the old one, so she'd worn her running one all the time instead, wearing off the rubber on the bottom. If she had her chukkas, she'd have been able to wear a pair. That would look better than a shoe and a rubber-soled sock. Well, not with the dress skirt and silk tank, but still...

"You haven't been authorized to leave!" The over-muscled nurse screamed from the cement steps.

"I don't need authorization to leave. I can leave whenever I want. I'm not a full-time patient. I haven't been committed!" She jerks the car door, realizing when she almost dislocates her shoulder and elbow that it is still locked. Pulling the keys from her pocket, she punches the button with her thumb and scrambles into the car, kicking the shoe off and tossing it to the passenger side floor. For all her bluff that she doesn't need approval to leave, she isn't certain it's true.

The nurse stands on the wide concrete sidewalk, staring and glaring, arms crossed.

Mel doesn't care. They aren't helping. Talk is just talk. It doesn't solve anything.

Punching and screaming at the doctor isn't helpful, either, but Mel doesn't want to think about that. Not right now.

Right now, she's thinking of her mother, the woman who raised her and wiped her tears and soothed her hurts. Soothed most of them anyway.

A major hurt had just had the scab ripped off—a scab she'd thought had healed to a scar. Her father was dead—dead for almost a year now. That's what Glenne had said last night. Her best friend had gotten off the phone with her own mother, who had dropped it like a reminder—but Glenne hadn't known. Mel trusts Glenne to tell her the truth. Always had, always will.

The Manleys didn't like to announce their family news. Brad probably put a small announcement in the paper and let their mother hold an even smaller service; Mel could see, in her mind, an imaginary wooden urn of his ashes sitting stop the mantle in the living room of her childhood home.

Hell, the Manley family—her family—hadn't bothered to announce it to her. Had her brother tried to call? Had their father been sick? Was it a heart attack or stroke? Had someone finally taken him out after he'd pissed them off?

Granted, her father hadn't wanted to talk to her after she'd joined the Marines, had all but disowned her—hell, maybe he had—but shouldn't someone have told her he was gone?

Shrugging off the anger and old hurts, ignoring them when they stuck their claws back in to drag along behind her like a shadowed veil, she punched the steering wheel, fighting off tears. She couldn't drive if she was crying.

She and Glenne had done the blood-sisters pact back in middle school, in their palms not their fingers, making it all that much stronger—or so they'd believed back in sixth grade.

Why couldn't she trust her mother the same as she could her best friend? Surely her mother would have tried to call?

After all, she'd shared blood with her mother for nine months while she'd been in the womb. Shouldn't that count more than a shallow slice in her palm with a dirty jack knife washed off in the river?

Had the VA known? Was that, along with a diagnosis of PTSD, something they'd kept from her? She'd found that out this morning. After the brand-new prosthetic had been refitted as best it could, the foot still a little too big, her stumped knee not quite snug in the cup. The counselor had mentioned it like Mel already knew.

Mel shouldn't care. They were a bunch of white coats who didn't understand. They didn't understand what had happened to her. The doubt that riddled her thoughts, that stopped her from making a decision. What if she was wrong? What if she'd misread something? She couldn't talk to them about it. She'd tried, mentioned something casually, hoping it would lead to something more. But it never had.

Then there was the regular stuff that happened. The firefights, the dead bodies. Talking didn't help with that, either. Talking meant remembering, when all she wanted to do was forget. Remembering led to nightmares and no sleep, which led to anger and yelling—and drinking at home until she couldn't be angry and all she wanted to do was sleep—and then getting fired from her job.

Not that the job mattered. She had a disability pension that paid enough for her to live on. Maybe not well. Maybe not the way she'd like. But it bought groceries and paid rent to live in someone's basement, and her car insurance. The car itself was all paid up; she'd saved her money when deployed, buying the two-year old model outright off the lot upon her victorious return—alive but not well and whole—to the States.

The scream of tires is a satisfying balm on an otherwise crummy day. The sports car responds like a HUMVEE never could, turning sharp and fast and light.

The prosthetic is heavy and it's jammed up against the little slant of the car floor. Good thing her right leg is okay. She'd have a hell of a lot more speeding tickets if that had been the one she'd lost.

Mel is good now—well better, the rage ebbing—her anger unable to keep up with the car. As long as she doesn't get a speeding ticket. Another one would be more than her license could handle.

§

The recruiter had smiled and taken her papers, placing his own scrawling signature below hers. "All set. You should be scheduled for transfer to Parris Island in a couple of weeks, but I'll let you know the exact date."

"Okay. Thanks." Mel stood and held out her hand.

The recruiter took it, his fingers squeezing hers in a tight grip. "Good to have you on the team."

When Mel left, the sun was shining and the world was right. She wouldn't stay in forever, only long enough to earn a degree and see a bit of the world.

But the sun was gone when she got home.

"Get out!" She'd never heard her father scream like that, guttural and deep, gushing from a depth long hidden and far away. He held himself still, like if he moved he'd shatter and never be put back together.

Her mother held on to her father. Mel thought he might have taken a swing if she hadn't.

"Why?"

"No daughter of mine is going to war!"

Who said anything about going to war? Oh, sure, there was a chance. But she was in it for the education benefits.

"It'll pay for my degree!"

"You'll die first!"

"Can I get my stuff?"

"No! That stuff belongs to my daughter and you're not her." His pointing finger shook in front of her face.

Mel stared, not quite comprehending what was happening. She couldn't even get her clothes? Those items she'd bought with her own money?

"Come on." Glenne tugged on her elbow, backing away toward the old Cadillac behind them, steam still coming off the engine where the rain tapped the hood. "You can stay at my house tonight. Borrow something of mine to sleep in."

Stumbling, Mel followed her best friend to the car they'd borrowed from Glenne's parents to go into Richmond for the day. "Won't your parents mind?"

"Not when they hear what happened." Glenne backed up slow, the '85 Fleetwood longer than the little rusty bug she usually drove.

"I'm sorry you had to see that." Mel hunkered down in the passenger seat, wrapping her arms around her middle. She wanted to cry, the pressure building behind her yes, but something wouldn't let the tears fall.

"S'okay." Glenne stayed quiet, concentrating on the view out the windshield.

Mel thought her friend was trying to give her some time.

"He'll get over it. You'll see." Her voice was thick with conviction.

But Mel suspected he wouldn't. Her father didn't get over stuff. Once he made a decision, he stuck with it. That was the Manley way, after all. And this time—well, she'd never seen him like that. That wasn't the father she knew. Oh sure, he was strict and could yell, but today... She sighed and took in a drag of air.

"Your mom will talk him out of it."

Her mother had been shocked, too. Mel knew from the pallor of her face, the dark despair in her eyes. Her mother knew her father meant what he's said: Mel was no longer his daughter and nothing would change that. "We'll see."

Brad dropped a bag off the next day, giving it to Glenne's mother when the older woman opened the door.

"Don't you want to see your sister?"

"No time, sorry. Ma can only distract Dad for a little bit. I can't take too long or he'll know I've been here."

"He's still mad?"

"Yeah." Brad's voice was flat. He scuffed his toe and looked back to his car.

Mel watched from the window in Glenne's upstairs bedroom, tucked under the steep eave of the dormer. He didn't look behind to see if Mel was looking out, which she was. No silent wave. No shrug of "who knows why he did that." That's when the tears came.

She left for boot camp the following week, Glenne dropping her off at the bus station in Richmond for the ride south. Parris Island felt a world away, and in a way, it was. Her old life was already gone; the bus ride was just a trip through limbo.

"Take care." Glenne's eyes watered and she sniffed into her coat sleeve.

Mel nodded. "Sure."

"Write. Call. E-mail if you have a computer."

"I won't. Not in boot camp anyway." Mel's voice rasped, a whole pond of frogs having taken up residence in her throat the week since she'd signed the paper.

"Maybe you should-"

"No." Mel knew Glenne was going to suggest she revoke the contract. Explain what happened. But she couldn't. Well, she could. But something inside wouldn't let her. Besides, if she did, it was no guarantee that would pacify her father.

They'd talked about it every night over dinner, Glenne's parents patting her hand and telling her they were sure the Marines would understand.

But, why would they? Mel sure as hell didn't.

"I'll let you know where I'm stationed." The bus was only half full, other riders waiting to climb aboard. Mel stood at the end of the line, Glenne beside her.

"Someplace glamorous, I hope. Where you'll meet a suave gentleman who'll sweep you off your feet."

"I'm joining the Marines, Glenne. I'll be surrounded by men."

"I bet they aren't suave, though."

Mel laughed and the queue inched forward.

Glenne sighed. "I'm going to miss you."

"I'll miss you, too. But hey, you're going off to Duke anyway."

"Yeah, but..." Glenne's voice trailed off.

"Hey." Mel poked her with an elbow. "It isn't horrible, you know. Maybe I'll fail and they'll kick me out."

"You can do that?"

"Well, not on purpose."

Glenne's look conveyed the thought that maybe 'on purpose' would be a good thing.

"I'm not going to fail out on purpose. That's not me."

"Yeah." Nodding, Glenne embraced her in a swift hug. They were almost at the bus. "Take care of yourself."

"You, too."

And then she was gone, her long legs taking her blonde hair through the crowd waiting for the next bus, and into the station and away.

Mel had never felt so alone in all her life.

# 2

## SNAKE IN THE ROAD

The brown snake sunning itself on the narrow strip of asphalt affirms she's far from the roar of the city. Only on the least travelled roads would a snake dare to sun itself in the open like that.

Though Rt17 is well-traveled in summer, in the winter and fall months, most folks stayed with I95, unless they were specifically heading to Tappahannock or Saluda. And who did that in October? Not tourists.

The roads that veer off it are even less traveled. More so now than when Mel was younger, but they are still mostly single-laned, the edges jagged and washed out, no painted line to tell you where the middle of the road is.

Mel takes a breath and swings the little Miata to the left, glancing in the rearview mirror to watch the reptile flail itself into the tall reedy grass on the side of the road; she missed. The reeds quiver then still before she makes it around the next turn.

The sun is high in the sky—another reason for the basking serpent—and its glare makes her squint. For today, the sun still thinks its summer, and by mid-afternoon, the air could be as hot and muggy as deep August. She pulls the visor down; she doesn't want to wear her sunglasses. She isn't on vacation, and sunglasses are for the beach or a resort.

But, that sunning snake means she's getting close to the farm. She pushes the accelerator, less because she's in a rush to get there and more because she might turn around and head back. Though, to what, she's not sure. The six-month lease on her Woodbridge basement studio had expired and she'd moved her furniture into storage and the bulk of her clothes into Glenne's garage. What she'd brought with her, mostly jeans and t-shirts, are packed in two borrowed suitcases in the trunk.

Her uniforms, along with the medal no one saw her receive, were carefully folded and stowed in her standard-issue green duffel and put in Glenne's garage. Mel had worried that Rick, her husband, would mind, but he'd helped stuff the bag on the shelf next to his half-restored Corvette. Mel thought it was a Sting-Ray, but couldn't be certain, and she'd been too embarrassed to ask.

The old general store she remembers is boarded up, the edges of weathered plywood bowing away from one of the windows no one bothered to fix, but the lights are on over the gas pumps, so she pulls in. It is the last place to fill up the tank; her Dad used to fill gas cans to keep at home for emergencies.

Newer places have been built out on Rt17, bigger places with convenience stores and coffee bars in them, places where semis can pull over for the night when they don't want to use I95.

This place is a holdover, and it makes Mel feel old. Apart. *Distanced*. And yet, it is familiar, unchanged. A part of her and her past.

An old man shuffles out from the building, his overalls held up by only one latched strap, his undershirt stained and wilting. "What can I do fer ya?"

"I need gas." Mel climbs out of the little sports car and stretches. She shakes her left leg, loosening the cotton of her pant leg from the hinge, letting the extra length pool at her ankle. She likes the little car, the sportiness, the speed, but it's proving cramped for longer trips, even for her five-five frame.

Maybe it's the prosthetic that doesn't fit.

She flips open the tank lid and turns the cover.

The old man picks up the dispenser and puts it in, humming an old tune half under his breath. He pushes a button and squeezes the lever, watching the numbers on the meter increase. "How much?"

"Go ahead and fill it." Mel walks around the car, scuffing the toes of her old combat boots in the dirt, small steps to hide the limp. Rocks are mixed in with the dirt; new rocks with jagged edges. He must have just had a load brought in.

"Where ye headed?" The man narrows his eyes and looks her up and down. The look doesn't bother Mel, not like it would have in the city. Out here, he's just trying to figure out if she's lost.

"Manley farm."

"Way out there, huh?"

"Yup. Way out there." The farm is one of the last houses on the road, situated just after it turns from asphalt to dirt. Only the Mackinaws live farther down the dirt. Any farther, and you hit river. Then the road veers, following the edge of the water, until it finds pavement again.

"Visiting?"

"Maybe." Mel flicks her glance to the meter. It reads better than twenty dollars. It had only needed half a tank.

The pump stops and the old man tugs the dispenser out. "That'll be twenty-two fifteen."

Pulling a twenty and a five from her pocket, Mel hands it over, waving one hand when he starts to make change. "Don't worry about it."

"Don't like charity." He juts his bottom lip out and chews on his tongue.

"It isn't charity. I hate change in my pockets." Mel gets back in the car and turns the key.

"Manley's don't like visitors."

"I know. They don't like family, either." Smiling, ramming the gear shift into drive and stomping on the gas, she waves and spins back onto the road. Better to get there and get it over with.

§

It was a snake that got her, bursting from the dry crumpled grass on the side of the dirt track to grind its teeth into her left calf, above the top of her suede chukka. She'd screamed but kept a hold on her weapon, shaking her leg to dislodge the attacker, terrified she'd alerted an enemy of their presence.

It didn't matter.

Gunney obliterated the snake with a spray of machine gun fire; its blood spatter soaked her pant leg and clung to the skin beneath.

"Viper." The second lieutenant still had acne and outranked her. Not that anyone cared about the state of your skin in the middle of nowhere. "Better tie her leg off."

Gunney kept his weapon aimed at the pieces of snake steaming in the sun, while the second lieutenant and the major wrapped a tourniquet on her lower thigh. Two other infantrymen carried her back to camp, each with a broad shoulder under one arm, keeping her leg dangling to keep the venom-infected blood away from her heart. The bite throbbed and she sobbed every time her foot smacked the dirt.

"It's okay, Manley." Gunney walked ahead of them, with the Major, machine gun out and ready, her weapon slung over his back. "We're almost back at base. They got antivenin."

The new medic on duty, just out of corpsman school, turned a tepid green when he caught sight of her leg, the skin torn and red and oozing thick yellow pus. The skin was already peeling back and turning gray. He injected her at the site, above the bite and spread a topical anesthetic over it so he could cut off the already-dead skin.

Gunney stood nearby, watching them, his gun still out, his finger still at the ready. That was a steady state for Gunney; Mel figured the man might sleep with his machinegun resting on his chest. "You okay, Manley?"

"Yeah, I'm good." Mel stood up from the gurney, wincing when her body weight caused the bite to burn again. She wanted away—away from medical, away from Gunney, maybe away from Afghanistan.

"No, you ain't. You're staying here for the night." He nodded to the gurney and pushed her back down. Mel tensed at the touch but he didn't back away. "No sense dying from a snake bite. You can get one of them back in the states. No medal for that."

Forcing herself to relax, after all the nurse was watching, Mel sank back to the gurney, happy to have the throbbing ease. She swung her legs back up and lay back. In her now-cut away uniform trousers and t-shirt, she was comfortable and exhausted enough to sleep—even with her right boot still on.

The medic made her take the boot off, though, and whispered the passdown to the medic that took the night watch.

When Mel woke up next, the nurse wore a little paper cup on her head and spoke English with a German accent. "Ah, gut. You are awake finally."

Mel was awake, but the nightmare had started. Her left leg was gone, taken just below the knee.

§

A bump and the crunch of gravel mark the end of the asphalt. Mel half expects the county to have taken the pavement farther by now, so the spitting rocks come as a bit of a surprise. She wonders if had been her dad or Mr. Mackinaw that nixed the plan this time around. The plan to extend the asphalt had been put up decades ago; the bus drivers want it, the town wants it. But the Manleys and Mackinaws don't, so the asphalt stops right where it is.

Back when she was a kid, and still welcome in her parents' home, the county had tried to take the pavement farther, but both Manleys and Mackinaws had protested, and the commissioner had backed down. He'd had to: Jackson Manley had mentioned that the commissioner's son owned the company likely to do the paving, and Bernard Mackinaw had mentioned that the commissioner's daughter was married to the son of the commissioner of the next county over—where the next piece of asphalt road started.

Slowing the car, she watches for the driveway markings: the tin mailbox set on a tall stump driven into the ground, and the rusted No Trespassing sign on a metal pole. She finds them both, just around the bend, and edges the car onto the winding drive, more dirty rut than anything else.

A stream cuts through the property, winding through overgrown bushes and orgies of twisted trees. The old wooden bridge Mel expects to find crossing it is gone, replaced with a cement culvert and concrete pad. The car creeps over, and nothing creaks or bends, so Mel lets out a sigh and relaxes a little, letting the car guide itself by way of the ruts.

She passes a field, empty save for the big dead-looking tree in the middle. Only dead-looking, because the tippy-top branches sprout still-green leaves desperately reaching for the sun. It's been that way ever since Mel can remember, and the thick limbs, turned and gnarled as they are, holding her and three friends without fail, every summer.

Part of the fence is falling over, the wooden posts crooked, the barbed wire dangling in the grass. Tufts of reed and brush dot through the old hay, gone to seed without being cut and baled. A neighbor from up on the asphalt part of the road used to come down and cut it for free, taking half the bales back for his cows. She'll have to ask Mom why he hadn't done that this year.

The house nestles behind a short rise, the skinny dormers and even skinnier chimney rising from the metal roof visible. Faint smoke drifts from the brick stalk, faint gray in the otherwise blue sky. Mel winds the car around the rise. A late-model Impala is parked next to the door; an old F150 sits next to the woodshed, rust dusting the bottoms of the doors and fenders, the bed loaded with stacked wood, still fresh.

Beyond that is the barn, a calico cat sitting by its far corner licking its front paw. It glances up at the car but continues cleaning itself. Farther out, in the field behind the barn, a few lazy cows graze and swat at flies. There are three sheep in the field, too, as well as what looks like a llama, but Mel would have to ask to be certain.

Parking the car, she cuts the engine, staring at the odd beast. Tapping the steering wheel, she considers her options. Did she go to the door and knock, or walk in like she'd never been thrown out?

"Hello?" A woman stands in the door, holding the screen open, her head cocked to one side, examining the car. Her hair is white, the breeze whipping the curls around her thin face. Mel can't see the woman's eyes, but she knows they are blue—a blue identical to her own.

She pops open the car door and climbs out, balancing carefully on the left leg before the right one joins it, tucking her still-brown curls behind one ear. "Hey, Ma. It's Mel."

"Mel? Melanie Marie!" Her mother pushes, lets go of the screen door, and rushes out, hands twisting in the blue apron that covers her jeans. The screen door slams and bounces behind her, not quite fitting square in the frame.

Mel lets out a breath, relaxing and smiling and holding out her arms. Her mother reaches her, grabbing her close and squeezing tight. "Oh, it's so good to see you."

She squeezes back, pressing her lids shut tight to keep the tears inside. "I missed you."

"Oh, baby, I missed you, too." Her mother leans back, hands gripping her shoulders, tears drip off her cheeks. "I'm sure your father did, though he'd never say it."

Mel nods but says nothing, swiping at hot tears. She didn't like her mother's lie, but didn't dare call her on it. The man was gone and she'd never known it.

"I've been in touch with Glenne. She was talking to her mom and her mom mentioned it. Glenne told me. She hadn't known, or remembered, or whatever, but her mother thought she had, or something like that." Her mom wasn't the only one versed in little white lies.

Her mother nods and let's go. "I'm sorry you had to find out like that. I didn't know how to reach you."

There had been one call, after Mel woke up, after that last abbreviated tour in Afghanistan, from that hospital in Germany. The line had been scratchy, scrawling across the

Atlantic, but she'd needed to talk to her mother, to hear her voice and feel the comfort of her words, even from a distance. Needed to hear her mother say that everything would be okay—even without her leg.

Her dad had answered the phone and hung up at her first stammered word. She hadn't tried again.

"He was bull headed." Wrinkles form when her mother smiles, deep crinkles in her cheeks and temples.

"Yeah." Mel nearly chokes.

"So are you." Her mother pokes a finger into Mel's shoulder.

Mel shrugs it off and wipes at another tear. "Not as much as he was. Trust me."

"Are you staying for a while?"

"Am I invited?"

"Of course." Her mother sounds shocked.

Mel raises a brow at her mother. "Of course?"

"You're here. This is your home."

Nodding, Mel decides not to argue that she'd been kicked out and told in no uncertain terms that she was never to come back. After all, those words hadn't come from her mother's mouth.

Neither had any words to the contrary, and maybe that is why she'd only made two calls in fifteen years—the first after boot camp. Her mother could have always tried to call her back. No matter how far out from anywhere the farm was, it was the first to have a phone and an indoor toilet, the first to have a TV. Her father would have upgraded the phone to have caller ID.

And if she'd really wanted, she could have called the Marines. The recruiting office in Richmond would have helped her. Hell, the mayor would have been able to find her.

"I made bread today; the loaves are almost ready to go in the oven. I can make fry bread to go with dinner if you want." Her mother links their arms and tugs her toward the house.

Mel jogs to cover the stutter in her step. "What's for dinner?" It's Saturday—probably beans, greens, and pork.

"I've got navy beans and kale simmering in a pot with sausage and a bit of ham that was left over. So, soup."

Mel keeps in her snicker. Even with dad gone, some things would never change. "Fry bread sounds great, Ma."

She doesn't mention her leg and her mother doesn't notice. Mel isn't sure how she feels about that. Is she getting that good at walking with the prosthetic?

§

They were in the middle of fum-duck Afghanistan, canvassing, checking for insurgents, when the little girl offered them bread—small flat loaves cooked in outdoor ovens. The grain was coarse and nutty, and the warm, yeasty carbs filled Mel's stomach. The family offered stew, too, filled with vegetables and meat, the broth glossy with fat and leafy green herbs she couldn't name.

Mel dipped a piece of bread in the broth, letting all the goodness soak in. She was hungry, and didn't care if she'd tried being vegetarian back in the States. Over here, you took whatever food was offered and said thank you. You didn't ask what kind of meat or vegetable or where it came from.

They'd driven all day, the HUMVEEs, and personnel carriers and tankers, growling over the dirt, kicking up a dust cloud trail longer than the caravan. It was a show of force to people that already understood it; they were on the watch for those that didn't and wanted to test it.

The Quonset-hut base on the outskirt of US allied territory was behind them, this village one of many they passed through.

The men didn't like to look at them and the women wouldn't. It was only the children, who didn't understand who they were and what they carried in their trucks, who smiled and spoke.

Mel dug in her pocket for something to offer in return. She didn't have much, only a couple of coins she'd gotten as change from the gedunk after buying a Reese's Cup for three bucks.

Holding out the shiny quarter, she nodded at the young girl to take it. The child did, rubbing her fingers over the surface, running a grimy nail over the ridges on the edge. Grinning, the girl ran off, ducking into a brick home halfway to the brush, her sing-song voice calling back in words and tune that Mel could never understand.

**3**

## HOME AGAIN

Dinner is just as Mel remembers: sitting at the wide kitchen table, scarred by generations of Manley's cutting and kneading and eating off it. The table is nearly as big as the kitchen, and the mismatched chairs, the pale green paint worn off in places, fill the rest.

Mel remembers helping Ma paint the chairs one summer long ago; two of them came from the old Manley set, a couple from her mother's parent's set, and the rest from the antiques mall in Tappahannock. They'd painted the kitchen walls a similar green, and Dad and Brad had put new brown tiles down for the floor.

They eat at one end, close to the old 50s stove with the baking drawer; the tureen sits between them on an old, red hot pad, the fresh fry bread draining on paper towels on a cracked platter next to it. Ma had taken down the china bowls that had been passed down by her great-grandmother and the silverware reserved for Christmas and

Easter that Dad had bought for their anniversary the year before Mel joined the Marines.

Bright yellow placemats mark their seats. The soup is thick and rich, and a home-made peach pie has been taken from the freezer, waiting to be warmed up for dessert. There would be enough left over for breakfast.

"Well," Ma wipes her lips with a paper napkin and sets down her spoon, "tell me what you've been up to."

Mel tears a piece of fry bread, watching the trapped steam spiral up from the moist center. "I'm not a Marine anymore."

"Well, that's a good thing, isn't it?" Ma sits with her hands in her lap under the table, blue eyes trained on Mel's face.

Shrugging, Mel examines her food and tears off another piece of bread, coating this one with butter before popping it into her mouth. Not being a Marine is good in a way, but bad in another. How could she explain?

"I mean," Ma smooths over an invisible wrinkle in the placemat, her fingers shaky, "you won't be going off to fight again."

"Yeah, there's that." Mel leans back in her chair, ignoring the tell-tale shaking and her stomach-tightening response. "But it's all I can remember doing, training and fighting. I tried a desk job at Quantico, but I can't be inside all day like that. Not right now anyway."

Though the prosthetic meant most physically laborious jobs were out of reach, she'd hated sitting at that desk, staring at a computer screen filled with words and numbers and forms. It left her time to think, for thoughts she didn't want to have sneak in to her brain.

And she'd need to get up and walk around, *move*. Which meant the work on the computer wasn't getting done.

Office jobs were not for her. From having to talk to people all the time to the buzz of the fluorescent lights to the smell of burnt coffee—she just couldn't take it. She didn't know what the work meant. Why is needed to be done.

She needed purpose, to do *something*, keep her hands moving, *fix* something that's broken.

"Okay—so what are your plans?" Ma grins and bites into her bread.

"I don't have any yet. I thought I'd come for a visit, see how you're doing, see what the farm looks like after all these years."

Her mother laughs, the sound forced. "You make it sound like you've been gone forever."

"Sometimes, it feels that way." And it does. Though the years were not that many—only thirteen years in the service and two-plus out—it feels like a lifetime. She is no longer the girl she was when she left, and different from the soldier she became, something completely different now. The changes deep, penetrating, and volatile. Things new, things missing, not only her leg, but emotions, illusions, memories.

§

The hospital in Landstuhl was not like a hospital in the States. Not much privacy, doors left open, nary a curtain to be seen. The beds were narrow, though more comfortable than her cot.

She couldn't always understand the doctors and nurses; they spoke German unless the words were directed at her. It was like background noise, a TV playing for company, but she could not turn it off when she was ready to be alone.

What was left of her leg burned, wrapped tight in bandages, what she swore was her foot, numb. She'd catch the attention of a nurse, pointing at the appendage, and they would loosen the gauze, so pins and needles danced under the skin. There was no pain with it; they'd tapped a nerve above her knee to stop that. But it still felt missing.

And Mel would catch a glimpse of the red skin, the scars and stitches. It was odd, because she could feel the rest of her leg, an invisible weight. Those first days, only the sight of the amputated limb reminded her it was now missing.

Then it became a lie, that weight. She knew it wasn't really there, and finally the pain stopped at her knee. Her brain recognizing that the nerves farther down were gone.

It felt numb, until the pins and needles.

It was welcome, though. Better than the burning.

It was boring--tedious--at the hospital. She could walk around, her left leg swinging free, her forearms braced on metal crutches, her gait an awkward, limping shuffle. But she couldn't do it alone. She needed someone with her in case she fell.

She needed someone to piss with, someone to shit with, someone to watch her while she ate.

The other patients were in similar situations, though many much worse. Mel still had one leg. So many others did not. And it wasn't a fucking viper that took theirs.

At night, they screamed and moaned, trapped in their last battle. When the noise started, a rapid scuttle of rubber soles would respond, sinking a needle into someone's arm, stopping the screams.

Mel never got a needle; she made sure of it by never sleeping. She dozed and napped, but between the burn in her leg and the sounds from the other patients, she never fully slept, and that kept the worst of the nightmares at bay.

The thought of someone—a nurse or a doctor—with a needle filled with morphine that could render her thoughtless was scarier than any nightmare. It felt too much like losing control, like a quick jump off a cliff into nothing. She's much rather the gentle downward slope of alcohol and the lie of just one more. But she couldn't get that here.

# 4

## JUST A DREAM

After midnight, it starts. Mel recognizes it as a dream, but is powerless to stop it from happening. Like a bad B film—scratchy sepia and Army green with bad lighting—it rolls before her eyes. The women, the men, the dogs—all dead, blood trickling in the dirt, turning it rusty brown. Muffled gunfire, like her hands are over her ears, bullets ripping into the dirt, spewing dust and debris when they hit. All in slow motion.

Waking, catching the scream in her throat, choking on the terror, Mel stares up at the ceiling she knows is up there. A light flicks on in the hall, beams creeping under her door.

"Mel?"

"Hey, Ma." Her voice shakes, more whisper than anything else. "I'm awake. Sorry if I woke you."

The door creaks open and a dark silhouette stands between Mel and the light that makes her squint. "I was getting up to go to the bathroom. Are you okay?" The figure steps into the room and flips the light switch.

"Yeah. Or I will be in a minute." She closes her eyes, but can't hide the wetness leaking beneath the lids. They flutter back open and she meets her mother's sleepy gaze.

Her mother stands just inside the door, hand still setting on the switch. The older woman stares at the metal and resin contraption propped next to the bed. "Mel, what...?" She swallows. "Mel, what happened?"

"I had a nightmare."

"That's not what I mean." She shuffles forward, pointing.

That's not what her mother wants to hear. She wants to know about the prosthetic. Dragging in a breath, Mel swallows and clears her throat. "I can't talk about it, Ma. Not right now."

Ma nods and backs up, leaving the light on. "I'm here, sweetie. I'm right here." The door closes with a soft thuck behind her. In the distance, muffled by the echoes of ancient gunfire and screams, a toilet flushes and slippers scuff on the hall floor.

Focusing on those sounds, the closing of her mother's bedroom door and the low creak of her mattress when she resettles, stills Mel's frantic heartbeat and calms her rapid breaths.

Closing her eyes, Mel shudders and lets the tears free-fall. At least she'd woken up before seeing the little girl shot while dancing and singing.

Mel's late breakfast is a slice of peach pie, warmed in an oven that has also baked three-dozen cookies and two sweet breads—one banana spice and one ginger zucchini—now cooling on a rack next to the sink. She sits at the table, a steaming cup of black coffee at hand, staring at the slice on her plate.

"There's whipped cream for it if you want. I made it when I made the breads; we can have spice bread with whipped cream as a treat after lunch." Ma stands at the sink, looking out the window, up to her elbows in suds, washing the implements she's used.

She hasn't asked about the leg, yet.

Mel expects it at some point, but is happy for the immediate reprieve. A dull ache throbs at her temples, easing without the dreaded questions.

"Just the pie would work for me." Mel sticks a bite in her mouth, chewing and swallowing before taking a sip of the coffee. She is being too abrupt with her mother, but she can't help it. She's tired; too scared to go back to sleep after the nightmare, she'd lain awake until her mother's alarm had gone off and she'd heard her mother's soft footfalls descend the stairs.

She hopes her mother doesn't mention the nightmare. She's still not up to talking about it. Alcohol hasn't passed her lips for almost a month; that is an accomplishment of sorts, but Mel doesn't expect it to hold forever. She's gone a dry month before, but there is always a dream or a conversation, followed by the need to drown the memories.

She'd prefer to talk about the leg.

But her mother says nothing, simply eats her pie and motions for Mel to do the same. The coffee is good and strong, the cream tinged with extra milk fat from the cows. It tastes a little green, but Mel doesn't mind. To her tongue, it means fresh and reminds her of her childhood.

"The peaches from old man Harris?"

Ma smiles and nods. "Won't use any other peaches, though old man Harris doesn't run the orchard anymore. He got sick last year and some young man came in and runs it now. Not only peaches, either. Lots of different stuff."

Change. Mel doesn't like it. She wants everything the same—down to her Dad in his chair yelling at the evening news.

"Sick?"

"Cancer."

"Ah." Mel sips her coffee and takes another bite of pie, her tongue searching for a difference—a taste, a texture. Something tangible in the fruit to reflect the new grower.

But the peaches taste the same as she remembers.

She's disappointed, but isn't sure why. Shouldn't she be happy that the peaches are the same? She came home, looking for an escape to simpler times. Not to her childhood—that was too far gone to ever truly find—but a hint or sense of its innocence.

Finishing the slice of pie and her coffee, she considers her options. Should she stay? She'll only have more nightmares, wake her mother, be forced in time to talk about what happened.

Ma stands and nods at her empty plate. Smiling, Mel hands her mother the dirty dishes. They are placed in the sink and hot water run over them.

"So, what are your plans now?" Her mother, the mind reader.

"I'm not sure." With a finger, Mel traces a particular scratch in the table top—etched in the wood when she'd been helping her mother pare apples one fall. "Do you want me to stay for a while?"

Turning from the sink, red-checked towel in her hands, her mother stares at her. "Mel, of course I want you to stay. Not just for a while, but for however long you want. Longer even."

Mel stares back. "I have nightmares."

Her mother shrugs. "Okay."

"Bad ones."

"I'm used to that."

"Not like these. These are...what I saw." Mel swallows the rock in her throat and it hurts going down. "I can't talk about it."

Ma sits back down, folding the towel and placing it in a neat square on the table in front of her. "Mel, there's something you should see."

"What?"

"Let's take care of the animals, and then I'll show you." Ma stands and grabs her jackets from beside the door, shoving her feet into the too-big galoshes on the boot tray below. "Can you..."

She waves her hands at Mel's legs.

"Yeah, I can." Mel knows this drill and grabs the other jacket and puts the other pair of rubber boots on over her thick sock and resin foot in the rubber-grip stocking. There is comfort in the semi-familiar, and some of that innocence glimmers. "So, what's that thing in the field with the cows?"

"Oh, that's Herbert. He's a llama." Ma heads outside, the wind whipping at her open jacket so it flaps like a rag on a pole.

"Why'd he come here? We never did animals like that." Mel skips to catch up, hitching the left leg, feeling so much like the teen she used to be, she wants to laugh. Saturday mornings had always been she and her mother taking care of the animals while Dad and Brad went into town for feed and other supplies.

Ma snickers. "It was an accident."

"An accident?"

"Junie Barber got him; thought she'd try a bit of exotic farming. Only it kept biting her son. So, I took him in. I mean, poor thing had nowhere else to go."

"Her son? You mean Kendall?"

Ma nods.

"I can understand that. I always wanted to bite him. So, he still lives at home? Figures."

Laughing, they walk into the barn, falling into the old patterns. Ma goes for the hose to give fresh water, Mel heads for the bins, filling the feeding troughs with a mix of oats and corn for the cows, clover and sweet grass or the sheep.

"What's the llama eat?"

"A mix of what everyone else eats, plus an apple from the covered bucket." Ma's voice is muffled.

Covered bucket? Hands on hips, Mel looks around, finding an old wooden bucket with a metal lid perched on top. Removing the lid, she finds it full of wrinkled apples.

The llama backs away, tucking into the corner to watch her out of one eye. The cows don't mind her, stretching their noses for a soft scratch. The sheep do, too, though they can't be the same sheep as when she'd been a child, and she rubs the top of their heads, smiling down at their half-regrown wool.

"How much wool did you get this year?"

"Enough for a blanket. I sent it off and it should come back as a nice warm full size." Ma turns of the water valve.

"I thought I'd put it on the bed in the back guest room, what used to be Brad's bedroom."

Mel nods and hangs the pitchfork back up, leaning against the wall. "That the usual amount?"

"Yeah. I don't keep as many as I used to. Too much work for just me."

"But you took in the llama?"

Ma looks up and grins, shrugging so that the too-big jacket flops on her shoulders. "Like I said, it had nowhere else to go."

Straightening, Mel nods and grabs a shovel. Ma opens the back gate and lets the sheep out into the fenced field. The sheep dart out in a pack, hanging tight to one another, aligned almost to a step. Mel starts clearing the old straw and manure.

The cows are next, but they amble into the field, one at a time, ignoring the small crowd of sheep that crowd together near the shady lean-to.

Herbert-the-llama won't leave, even with Ma in the field, calling him, offering him another apple from the bucket. The long-necked beast sticks to his corner, watching Mel and the shovel.

"I don't think this is going to work, Ma."

Sighing, Ma nods and tosses the apple to the old bull, who snuffles the ground looking for the second-hand treat. "He's stubborn. I'll come back out after lunch. He should be out by then."

They leave his gate open.

Chores complete, more or less, they walk to the small coop to check the chickens. The hens squawk and the rooster struts. Ma sprays the ground inside the pen with seed.

"Do you still milk?"

"After lunch. Unless I need to head into town, then I do it earlier." Ma watches the chickens peck, the rooster keeping watch instead of eating.

Mel nods, arms crossed, watching the fat birds.

"You can grab the eggs if you want." Ma stands, feed bucket in hand, sprinkling more seed over the bare spots.

Grabbing a basket, Mel walks to the back and lifts the hinged roof that covers the roosting cubes. Warm eggs nestle in down filled niches, and she reaches in, taking up each egg in turn and placing it in the basket. "Lots of eggs here."

"Yeah. Always lots of eggs. Good thing I like them." Ma stands at the corner. The rooster fluffs his feathers and lets out a loud cackle.

Mel smiles. That is always her mother's answer to the amount of eggs.

# 5

## ALERT

It was the squawking of the birds that alerted them that someone was coming. The chickens scattered into the brush. Whoever it was, the birds didn't expect them to be friendly.

Birds were smart. Mel had always known, having been raised on the farm. But here, it was more important. They were alarms, like dogs and trip wires.

The kids ran, ducking into the dingy huts and barns, seeking cover. They, too, knew to pay attention to the birds. Their mothers were already inside, their fathers standing, listening, tense and waiting.

Gunney had his gun out—of course—but everyone else had to grab theirs and brought them up. They backed up to each other, each facing a slightly different direction.

Mel held her breath and bent her knees. Her heart sped up, her breathing got shallow. The pant of the soldier next to her was harsh in her ear; she thought it was the Major, but couldn't dare to look and make sure.

That second could cost her.

Could cost everyone.

It was a flock of sheep and goats herded by a couple of young boys from the next town. They were avoiding their usual pass, probably due to it being occupied, but they wouldn't say that much.

The interpreter shrugged and Gunney motioned them to keep going, and so they did, the sheep and goats oblivious to the tension, skipping in the dirt.

Soon, the birds resettled and the kids came back out to play, only now the mothers followed them, bringing their chores with them, sitting outside to keep watch. The men also returned to their work, but stayed close to home.

Mel didn't put her gun down.

§

Inside, jackets hanging by the door and washed boots dripping on the tray, Ma makes a fresh pot of coffee. "We might need this after."

"After?"

"After I show you." Ma frowns and stares at the dripping liquid, tapping her fingers on the counter.

"Ma?" A knot forms in Mel's stomach. This isn't something she wants to know.

"It's not bad. It's...I wish your Dad had told you himself." Grimacing, Ma motions for Mel to follow and she does, shuffling, arms crossed. "It's why...well...why I couldn't take your side in that last fight. I wanted to, sweetie. I really did, but I couldn't. He needed me more."

Mel swallows, unable to nod or say it's okay. They head upstairs, to the hall outside the bathroom, and Ma pulls down the stairs to the attic, the hinges creaking from disuse. Dust sprinkles down, like the first dusting of snow in the winter.

"Been a while since you've been up here?" She's hoarse and fights with her throat to let the words escape.

"Yeah." Ma starts up, stopping half-way to the top to pull the light switch. "Haven't had a reason to come up."

"But the Christmas stuff is up there."

"I wasn't up to Christmas last year. Maybe this year—if you stay—we can put it up."

It takes Mel extra time to ascend the narrow stairs, ensuring the false foot is secure before trusting her weight on it.

Ma waits at the top, patient as always, watching, a slight frown dipping her brows. It disappears when Mel reaches the top.

The attic is full of dust more than anything else, a thick layer of it obliterating sharp corners, blurring shapes one into the other.

"It's over here." Ma picks her way over the loose flooring. "Behind the baby furniture."

"I'm surprised you didn't give that to Brad when he and Chrissie had the baby." The crib is old and ornate, having been in the Manley family for a century or more.

"They were concerned that it wasn't safe, so they got something new." Ma edges her way around a box and squats in front of a trunk. It isn't locked, but the clasp sticks and Mel helps her pry it open. It squeals a protest that rings in Mel's ears.

Inside, is an old Army uniform, the ribbons over the breast pocket faded and dusty but still straight. There are photos and a folder, a few yellowed pages sticking out.

"This is why your father didn't like that you joined the Marines. He knew what it meant." She strokes the uniform.

"Dad was in the Army?" Next to her mother, Mel settles on her right knee, the prosthetic too awkward for such a pose, so it remains stretched out to the side. Her hand reaches toward the dark green fabric, not daring to make contact. It hovers, disembodied, in the space between Mel and it.

Ma nods. "He got out before we got married. We weren't dating until after his stint. Kyle got the farm and your father had no other option. Then, he came back, tried a regular job. That didn't work out so well, either--though we were seeing each other by then. When Kyle decided the farm wasn't for him, your Dad took over."

Mel stares at her mother. "Uncle Kyle gave the farm to Dad?"

"Yes, Uncle Kyle gave up the farm. Didn't tell your Dad, at first. Then your Dad came and never left." Ma sits on the floor, not minding the dust, tucking her legs to one side. "Your Dad saw action, none of it good. He had nightmares, too."

The tears surprise Mel. She didn't think she had any inside her, but they came, in rushes and sobs, dripping off her chin. "Why didn't he tell me?"

"He never said, but I think he thought it was too late. That he should have told you sooner to keep you out, and that if he told you after, it would make it worse."

Nodding, Mel swipes her cheek and sucks back the snot.

"Here." Her mother always has a handkerchief, and now is no different. She holds it out, folded, crisp, pristine.

It seems a shame to dirty it, but Mel can't breathe through her stuffed nose, so she takes it and blows. The sound echoes in the rafters, stirring more dust to dance around them.

"Where did he serve?"

"Vietnam. He enlisted as soon as he came of age." Ma reaches out and pushes damp hair behind Mel's ear. "He was in for seven years, got out two years after the end of the conflict. He got hurt; that's where his limp came from. He never told me much, but some of his friends died. I think he blamed himself."

His limp; Dad had always said he'd got it playing football in high school. Mel had never questioned that; neither had Brad. Her mother had never said anything different; why questin his story?

Mel picks up a photo, its edges worn and frayed. It shows a man, bare-chested with an arm slung over the shoulder of another man in a t-shirt and camouflage pants. Palm trees arch behind them, a single headlight from a Jeep in the corner of the frame.

"That's your Dad." Ma points to the bare-chested soldier. "That's when he was a layover for training in Hawaii. He was in the Philippines for a bit, too, at the end. You might have a sibling or two over there. I'm not sure. Like I said, we never talked about it much."

"Siblings?" Mel chokes. The idea that her Dad might have other kids, with someone other than her mother, is hard to stomach. "How?"

Her mother raises a brow and snickers.

"You know what I mean." But the mood lightens and it's okay because Ma seems okay with it. Or at least accepting.

"Yes. Your dad and I weren't together until he came back. I don't think he felt he could go back, for them or anything else."

"So, he just left them?"

"I'm not sure he left anyone. I got the feeling sometimes, that there was someone. Maybe just a girl. Maybe just a place. Maybe someone who died."

"Oh." Mel sets the photo back in the trunk and picks up another. It shows a man in his dress uniform, posing in front of an American flag. "Can I keep this one?"

"Sure." Ma touches a finger to the corner. "That's a nice one."

They close the trunk and head back downstairs, Mel taking her time, as much for composure as safety. The aroma of fresh coffee reaches her nose and her stomach grumbles.

Ma laughs. "I think it's time for the spice cake now."

"Maybe." Mel stops by her bedroom and sets the photo by the lamp, propping it up. She'll have to buy a frame for it tomorrow. See about making a copy, a bigger one that she can hang on the wall. Get one for Mom and one for Brad, too.

Damn. Brad probably doesn't know. Should she tell him? Should Ma? Did it matter?

Shaking the thoughts away, she descends the stairs.

In the kitchen, her mother has the coffee on the table, and two mugs, with the creamer in the carton and the sugar bowl next to it all. "Do you want whipped cream?"

"Yes." Mel sits at the table and pours two cups. "What are you going to do this afternoon?"

"Check that Herbert is in the field, clean out his stall and milk the cows." Ma adds her cream and sugar and sips her coffee. "Then, I'll watch my shows on the TV and make dinner. What do you feel like eating?"

Mel shrugs. "I'm not picky." The spice cake is decadent, moist and spicy, and the whipped cream is cool and sweet. "Though, I could do with more cake for dessert."

"It was your Dad's favorite, too."

For the first time in a long time, a comparison to her dad doesn't hurt. It's a bit surprising. She'd never liked anyone telling her she did something like her dad. Not her mother. Not her uncle Kyle. Certainly not Brad, and whenever he had, the interactions had dissolved into a fistfight.

She's not sure she likes that it doesn't hurt. The fact that her father had served didn't change the horrible things he'd said, that he'd kicked her out of her home. The hurt meant he'd been in the wrong and she'd been in the right. If she'd been wrong, she was the one owing an apology.

And her dad isn't here for it.

§

Gunney and the Major were having an argument. They argued any time they weren't in a combat situation, or on the verge of one. Gunney had been in a long time, was almost ready to retire. The Major liked to pull rank, but even being a Major, in comparison to Gunney, he was new to service—hell, everyone in the unit was a newbie when compared to Gunney.

And Gunney didn't like when someone pulled rank.

So, they'd argue.

And this time, the Major went too far, and took a swing.

He missed of course, because Gunney ducked.

But Gunney changed in that instant, the look in his eyes darkening, his lips curling into a sneer. He crouched, looking the Major up and down. "You been drinking?"

"Course not. I'm sober as a Priest."

"How many Priests do you know? And how well do you know them?" Gunney cocked his head and wagged his brows. "I'm Baptist, so I'm not that intimate with them."

"Son of a bitch." The Major swung again, missed again.

Gunney laughed, which didn't help diffuse anything.

"Hey, guys." Mel stepped forward, one hand raised. "I don't think-"

But the Major swung again, his fist glancing against Mel's shoulder, and she staggered forward.

"Oh, you little shithead." Gunney straightened, set Mel aside, and wound up, his punch making solid contact with the Major's jaw.

Spittle hit Mel's face, she was so close. "Gunney, this isn't-"

The Major swore and touched his cheek. It was already swelling, blood trickling from a cut on his lip. He bounced in place, raising boxer's fists. "Come and get me, old man."

Eyes narrowed, Gunney waited.

Mel's stomach clenched and she swallowed. "Guys, he isn't worth the kp duty."

Hell, they were already in trouble. Gunney had hit a higher-ranking officer. That would not go well with the new LtCol. The new man-in-charge of their unit already

didn't like Gunney.  It might be past basic kp duty pub-
lishment already.

Another swing from the Major, and Gunney dealt the final blow, breaking the man's nose. The Major hit the floor hard, his head smacking the packed dirt floor of the makeshift garage.

Mel knelt beside the man, checking his pulse. It was weak.

"We need a medic, Gunney."

Gunney stood, breathing hard, face flushed, staring down at them.

"Gunney!"

"Fine." The older Marine lunged forward to the closest HUMVEE, snatching up the radio and making the call. A moment later, he slammed the mic down. "They're on their way."

"That wasn't smart."

Shrugging, Gunney paced away. "What are they going to do?"

"You're too close to getting out to screw up." Mel checked over the Major's head. She couldn't see any blood, so he should be okay. "The LtCol is looking for a way to get to you."

"I'm not worried. He was out of line and swung first." Gunney swept a hand toward the prone Marine.

"I don't think the LtCol is going to care about that."

A door slammed and two medics rushed in, bags out, another two unloading a stretcher to bring through the wide end.

"What happened?" The first medic squatted down and checked the Major's pulse.

"He took a swing at me and I hit him back."

Mel groaned. Leave it to Gunney to spit that out all at once."

"He started it?" An MP had come in with the stretcher, and stood, one hand on his hip next to his pistol.

"Yup." Gunney nodded. "I wouldn't have finished it, but he wasn't careful and tagged her." Gunney jerked his head in Mel's direction.

Damn. Why did he have to bring her into it?

But she nodded. That *was* when Gunney had started hitting back. "He's telling the truth."

"What happened?" The MP pulled out a notepad and flipped to a blank page. He looked at Mel, one brow raised.

The medics lifted the Major onto the stretcher and carried him out.

Mel watched them leave. They weren't especially careful with the officer. Maybe they were familiar with his reputation.

Sighing, she shook her head. "It was just verbal shit, like usual, and I tried to stop them. Made the mistake of stepping between them, and the Major wound up and caught me on the shoulder."

The MP scribbled in the pad, nodding. "Uh huh. Finally came to blows."

"That Major is an ass." Gunney's interjection wasn't going to help.

"Doesn't mean you get to hit him." The MP looked up and directed a pointed look at Gunney.

"He would have hit me. Hell, he swung first."

"And if he had made contact first, he would be the one answering my questions and looking at possible Brig time."

"He'd never make it in the Brig. And the LtCol would never put him in. Damn officers stick together like shit in the winter."

The MP sighed and slammed the notepad shut. "I'll see what I can do for you, but this might be the kicker, old man."

"Yeah, yeah." Gunney waved him off. "Tell me if the Major doesn't wake up. *So, I can celebrate!*"

Flipping his middle finger at Gunney, the MP sauntered to his Jeep. "I'll keep you informed."

# 6

## SUPPLY RUN

"This is all you need?" Mel reviews the short list of feed supplies for the animals.

"Yeah. Brad brought most of what I need Wednesday."

"He usually do that?"

"No. His visit included an attempt to convince me to sell the farm and move into town. He's got an in-law suite at his house. Had it built on before Tilly had surgery and stayed with them for a while after." Ma wears her jacket and boots again.

"Tilly is Chrissie's Mom?"

"Aunt." Ma stamps her feet in the boots to push them all the way on.

"You sure you don't want help?" Mel is unsure about going into town. Any excuse not to would make her happy.

"Mel, I do this every day. I'm fine. Go into town and get the supplies. Oh, and you could buy some steaks at the grocery store and say hello to your brother."

"Do I have to?"

"Yes."

Groaning, Mel leaves with the keys to the truck. Though it's a short list, there's no way she's putting it in her Miata; she doesn't want the trunk smelling of fishy oats.

"The extra gas can is in the truck box." Ma calls from the barn.

It takes Mel four tries to start the truck, and when the engine rumbles to life, it makes the whole vehicle shake. She guns the engine until the rumble subsides.

The truck isn't the size of a HUMVEE, but she's been driving nothing but the Miata since she got back—sleeping in it one month—so it feels huge on the road. She's happy she doesn't meet any other cars, or she might have a close-up with the ditch.

The feed supply store is exactly where she remembers it, with the hardware store across the street next to the now-abandoned lumber depot. The train tracks, mostly unused now, once brought lumber in. Nothing brings it in now; folks drive into Richmond if they need anything, or have it delivered.

The kid at the register is young, which doesn't surprise Mel. She stares and cracks her gum when Mel pulls out the list from her mother. Smiling, Mel hands the paper over. "For Manley farm."

Nodding, the kid takes the list and hollers to someone in the back. It's another kid—a boy this time, his hair cropped close to his scalp, with muscles and some height on him—and relays the list, punching buttons on the cash register at the same time.

"The truck is up front."

"Sure. Gimme me fifteen." The boy nods and heads to the back.

"Thanks." Mel hands her credit card to the girl, who takes it and frowns.

"This is Mrs. Manley's order."

"I know; the card is mine."

"You're paying?"

"Yes."

The girl shrugs and swipes the card. "I'm gonna need your zip code."

Mel recites the needed info and signs the receipt.

"Thanks."

"You're welcome."

Outside, the last bag is loaded into the truck bed and the boy slams the gate shut, yanking it to make sure it locked. "You're good."

Mel smiles and shakes the kid's hand, slipping him a ten-dollar bill.

The kid grins and offers a half-handed salute. "Tha-a-ank you."

Rolling her neck, Mel climbs into the truck and considers her next stop. The grocery store is down the block, across from the gas station. Ma wants steak and a polite how-do conversation with her brother.

The steak is doable. Mel isn't sure about the conversation.

But she is a Marine, though she no longer wears the uniform. She can do this.

Starting the truck, she puts it in gear and rolls out. There's still no stoplight, not even a blinking yellow-red one at the single intersection. It's still a four-way stop that everyone ignores.

§

The personnel carrier stopped and the abrupt lack of movement jerked Mel from her semi-doze. "Wha-?"

"Don't know. Get ready." The driver was older, another Sergeant with experience.

Mel jerked up, grabbing her machine gun from its safe-stowed position and rested the barrel on the bottom of the window. Sleep was gone, like it never had been, replaced with a rush of adrenaline. "Where are we?"

"Three miles from base." The driver had a pistol in one hand, raised and ready to use, the other hand gripped tight to the wheel.

Their truck was loaded with food and a few office supplies, but the truck behind was loaded with ammo. In the side mirror, a swarm of Marines surrounded that truck, weapons pointed out, ready.

Someone honked and the vehicle ahead of them—carrying medical supplies—started forward. They followed, as did the truck behind, though the Marines stayed outside, weapons still ready.

Holding her breath, Mel used her sight, crouching, on one knee in her seat. Outside was nothing but sand and shrubs and rocks. Something moved—a sway of branches—and a spray of bullets erupted from behind, obliterating the dried leaves and limbs. A hare jumped out and scampered off.

Mel let out the breath she was holding, her lungs straining to take in silent air. Sweat crept into her eyes, stinging. She blinked it away, shaking away the hair that blocked her view.

The caravan continued, inching forward. Mel kept a lookout, but nothing moved. No barrage of ammo spewed from behind.

The radio crackled and a broken voice filled the cab. Mel ignored it, paying attention to the landscape. It wasn't her job to listen to the radio.

"Looks like a false alarm." The driver set his pistol on the seat, but didn't stow it away.

Mel kept her gun out, too, and the Marines behind didn't load into the last truck to ride back. Each truck continued its inching momentum, all three miles, until they were inside the 10-foot chain link fence that marked the outer perimeter of base.

§

The parking lot at the grocery store is only half full. It is still too early on Saturday for most folks to be out shopping; around here, there are chores to be done first. The truck isn't easy to maneuver, so Mel parks it as best she can, but the driver-side tires edge over the white line into the next space.

She gets some stares. Folks recognize the truck, but not her. Oh, maybe they think she looks familiar, but can't quite place her. Or they do recognize her, but don't know what to say after all these years.

If she wanted, she could drive all the way into Tappahannock, to the Wal-Mart. But Brad doesn't work there. And it would be a waste off gas just for a steak.

A single register has a cashier working, a small line of folks waiting to check out. They aren't anxious, though, and talk and laugh while they wait. The fresh food area is meager, mostly local produce. Mel grabs a head of lettuce, a cucumber, and a tomato, setting them in a hand basket. There are green onions, too, so she picks up a bunch. She can put the leftovers in an omelet in the morning.

The meat is in the back, so she checks for steaks, picking up two packages, each with two thick slabs inside. She was vegetarian once, making her mother cook two versions of everything to satisfy her teenage attempt to save the animals, but that hadn't lasted long in Afghanistan.

"Melanie?"

She wonders, for a second, who told him she was here. No, wait. If someone had told him, he'd stay in his office. She looks up, forcing her lips to curl upward. "Hey, Brad."

"What are you doing here?" There is a bit of gray at his temples, heavy scruff along his jaw indicating he's growing out a beard for the winter. He's heavier than when she last saw him, but it's flab, more fill. His brown eyes are dark, like Dad's, but he has Ma's nose and cheeks.

"Visiting Ma. I'm allowed, I think."

"Well, yeah. But you haven't been back for, how many years?"

Mel nods and shrugs. "Dad told me to get out. I got out. Stayed out."

"And you're back?"

"Visiting. I heard Dad had passed away." Mel stares at her brother, satisfied when a dull flush of red spreads across his face.

"I didn't know your number or I would have called. I would have." Brad shuffles his feet and looks away, a tell-tale sign that he might not have. "Chrissie tried to track you down."

Mel isn't sure about that. Chrissie and Mel had never gotten along, never had anything in common, other than Brad, and that hadn't been enough to bridge any gap. "I moved around a lot." She guesses she can give him that and pulls her cell from her purse, shooting him a pointed look.

She's surprised when he pulls out his own phone and recites his number so she can put it in hers. She provides her own, and he punches it in. "I'll let Chrissie know you're home. You can come for dinner, bring Mum into town."

"That would be nice." It wouldn't be. Mel has never liked Chrissie. They'd been in the same class in high school, and Chrissie had been a bitch to anyone that didn't fall at her feet in awe of her beauty. Probably is still a bitch. Bitches don't change.

"I'll call and let you know." He tucks his phone away. "Look. I'm happy to see you. Happy you're home. I mean, *home*, you know."

"Okay." Mel stares. She didn't know what he meant.

He seems to understand that. He swallows and wraps an arm around her, pulling her close. "Ma was scared you wouldn't make it back."

Stiffening, Mel isn't sure how to react. She can't remember the last time her brother hugged her. Punched her, poked her, smacked her—yeah. Their childhood had been a long line of physical altercations. So, this is different.

She winds her own arm around him, awkward, squeezing back. "I am mostly."

"Dad, too. We talked once. He figured he'd blown it with you."

"He did." Mel shrugs away, trying to give him a smile but knowing it doesn't work. "Did you know he was in the Army?"

"What?" Brad looks shocked.

Mel nods. "Ma showed me a trunk this morning, up in the attic, with his uniform and some photos."

Shaking his head, Brad looks away. "I never knew. I mean, he told me not to join and all, but..." he swallows, "he never said anything about that."

"Yeah. I wasn't sure to believe it, but there are photos and stuff."

Brad tucks his phone back in a pocket. "Look, I gotta go back to work."

"Okay. Talk to you later." Mel backs away, her left foot lagging so she staggers but catches herself. Brad doesn't seem to notice, or doesn't understand the significance. She offers him a weak wave.

He raises a hand back and ducks through a door.

Well. That's that.

But is it? *Would* he talk to Chrissie about inviting her in for dinner? Probably, since he'd also mentioned Ma. But would Chrissie agree? How could she not? Mel is Brad's sister. There is no way to deny her.

"Mel?" The voice is male and husky, and it sends a little thrill down her spine. That voice always had. Even before it dropped two octaves at the start of high school.

"Ozzie." Mel turns and there he is: six-foot plus of muscle. Light-brown hair buzzed at the nape, longer with a natural spike on top, short beard just a tad shaggy—just enough to be extra morning-after sexy.

"I wasn't sure it was you." He has his own shopping basket and places it at his feet.

"It is." Mel shifts her basket to the other arm, smiling, though her teeth grit behind her lips. She glances at his left hand; a gold band glints on his ring finger.

Ozzie Harris had been her crush—hell, he'd been everyone's crush—all through middle and high school—and beyond if she is willing to admit it. He looks good—really good—and a small part of her hums.

"I heard you signed up?"

"Marines. Yeah."

"I also heard you saw some action."

Mel nods and glances at the shelf of canned tomatoes behind his left shoulder.

"You okay?"

"Okay?" She forces her eyes to meet his.

He shrugs. "I'm a firefighter. I've seen some stuff, though probably not like you. So, yeah, you okay?"

Oh, shit. This is not what she expects from him. He'd been the ultra-jock every-girl's fantasy cad. Why had he grown up into a nice guy?

Taking a breath, Mel makes to nod, but something stops her. Instead, she shakes it once. "But I'm working on it."

"Good." Ozzie shifts and crosses his arms, the ring flashing her. "If you need to talk..."

"Yeah. If I need to talk." She's heard that offer a thousand times. From nurses and doctors, the shrink at the VA, a new—now old—attempt at a boyfriend who didn't really listen when she'd finally tried it.

"Or not. I see a guy just this side of Richmond once a month. But, you know, if you want to go for a long run, or something. Burn off all that sharp energy."

Burn off energy...*sharp* energy. "I might take you up on that." Could she run in the prosthetic? She has one just for that purpose, but hasn't used it outside of walking on a treadmill or on an elliptical during therapy.

He tugs his phone out of a back pocket, calling her attention to the snug denim across his hips.

Damn. There is no way she'd make it through a run with him.

"Can I get a phone number?" Ozzie waits, finger poised on his phone.

"Sure." For the second time in ten minutes, she gives someone her cell number.

"Want mine? In case you need to call?"

"Yeah." Mel fumbles the basket, almost dropping it before snagging her own phone. She taps the number he recites to her onto the screen, not bothering to type his name. Her phone only has five numbers in it: Glenne's, which has been in it since she found her on Facebook a year ago; the number to the farm, though she never calls it; the number to her shrink at the VA, also a number she never calls; Brad's, only just put in; and now Ozzie's.

She could put his name in later, when she is thinking clearly. No way she'll forget whose number it is.

Ozzie stoops to pick up his basket. "Talk to you later, 'kay?"

Mel nods. "Sure. I'm staying for a bit."

"That's good. I think your mother could use the help."

Backing away, no glitchy near-trip this time, Mel waves and makes a beeline for the nearest cashier. Her limp is exaggerated, but she needs to get out. She needs air, and space. The walls are closing in, trapping her breaths. Her muscles twitch, choosing flight rather than fight, which is a good thing since her brain has shorted out, controlling her movements on autopilot.

The girl at the register rings her up without looking at her, and Mel swipes her card without looking at the total. She takes the receipt and grabs the two plastic bags. "Thanks."

The girl doesn't answer; she's ringing up the next customer.

And that's okay, because Mel is already out the door and jog-hopping to the truck, the prosthetic pinching the skin at her knee. Tossing the bags to the passenger side floor, Mel jumps into the cab and slams the door. Gasping, she rams the key in the ignition and guns the engine.

Tires squeal. She makes it out of the parking lot and out of town, roaring down the old road and back toward the farm. She stops for gas at the boarded-up station, the old man once again not wanting her change.

She takes it this time. She can't voice the words to tell him to keep it.

# 7

## HAVING FUN

Laughter.

Gunney could always make her laugh. Over beer. Eating pizza. Kissing. Doing more than kissing.

She'd thought, once, that Gunney was *the one*. He wasn't. Never would be. Not now.

Not ever and never had been. She knew that now.

But then...then he could also piss her off in less time than it took for a bullet to career out of the barrel of her machine gun. But they never fought. She never gave him the satisfaction of yelling at him; she'd turn around and leave.

And he would let her.

No one knew, or at least let on that they knew. She was a junior noncom, and any relationship was considered fraternization in the military--a definite "do not do". Of course, when you were at war, there were a lot more important problems for everyone to worry about.

Like whoever fed the military dogs table scraps. It wasn't healthy for them. And some could make them sick. The base vet was up in arms, and Mel understood why. Having been brought up around animals, seeing them suffer and not know why, she had some experience.

But that was minor compared to the issue of whoever was shirking their duties at restocking the ammo. Gunney was tracking it, watching the duty bill, shuffling Marines through each watch, closing in on isolating the single Marine that was always 'working' before the shortfall was discovered.

It made him edgy, combative. He fought with everyone. Even on the phone with his wife.

Mel had known he was married; he'd been open about that from go. But she also knew the relationship was in trouble. Gunney was always bitching about how she bitched at him. How she spent money they didn't have on stuff they didn't need. How she kept a boyfriend on the side. He had kids, but Gunney never talked to them when he called home.

The wife threatened him with divorce and never seeing his kids again. He'd slammed the phone down and buried his head in his hands.

Not knowing what to do, Mel had backed away from the door. She'd been going to try to call her mother, had gotten the courage up to try to wish her and Dad a happy anniversary. It didn't matter, though; they probably wouldn't answer, anyway.

She'd followed him when he left, talking to him. He never knew; he hadn't heard her. Had stalked away too fast for her to keep abreast of him. He'd been too angry to notice much of anything.

At medical, she stopped following. Gunney had met up with one of the nurses, a pretty petite blonde that most of the guys had wet dreams over. It seemed Gunney didn't have to dream, and they'd dropped their bottoms and fucked on an empty gurney prepped for an emergency, but kept in the storeroom.

Eventually, Gunney had tracked down the slack Marine and the ammo had been squared away ever since. The Marine had served a weekend in the Brig and two weeks on restriction, no longer allowed anywhere near the ammunition depot, but on regular, daily latrine duty.

"What's wrong?" Gunney whispered into her ear in the mess. Mel was waiting for what served as pizza and salad in the desert. It was food, but only just. If there was an alternative, she'd take it.

"Nothing."

"You haven't been by lately."

Mel shrugged and moved on down the line, a limp piece of cracker dough and burnt cheese on her plate next to wimpy greens already soaked in Italian dressing. She chose canned pudding--the flavor didn't matter, it all tasted the same--and a bottle of water.

"So, something's wrong."

"Why don't you go ask your nurse?"

"Nurse?"

"I saw you after you fought with Natalie." Mel walked to an already full table, forcing the Marine on the end to shift in and make room.

"That was-"

"I know what it was. It's not what I want." Mel opened the bottle of water and took a short sip. How could water taste like shit straight from the sealed bottle?

"I never offered more." Gunney growled, leaning over her, pushing his face into hers.

"Yeah." Mel snorted. "But I didn't realize you were offering it to everyone." She picked up her fork and started on the salad. The conversation was done and she wanted Gunney to leave.

But he didn't. He poked the shoulder of the Marine across from her, who slid over and let him sit down.

Mel sighed. This wasn't going to be pretty. "Just. Go. Away."

"No. Why are you punishing me?"

"I'm not. I'm just not having sex with you anymore."

The Marine next to her stopped eating and choked. The one next to Gunney stared.

Gunney stood and shoved at the table, making drinks spill and Marines grab their trays. He stomped away, uncaring of stares and whispers.

She probably should have kept her mouth shut. If the rumors spread too much, to too many ears, he'd get in trouble. Big trouble. The LtCol would have his ass in a sling and be happy about it.

She'd be in just as much trouble. Might be now.

"You really sleeping with Gunney?"

It was tempting. Though she shouldn't feel betrayed, she did, and it hurt. She could let it go, say yes, and watch him burn.

"Naw. I'm not stupid. That would be my career, too. I just wanted him to leave me alone. He's bitching about me not taking watch seriously." Mel shoved the pizza in her mouth and chewed, taking her anger out on the hapless dinner. "I figured that would shut him up long enough I could eat in peace."

The Marine across from her stared a moment before resuming his own meal. The one next to her took her at her word and grunted. "Smart girl."

Across the table, the other man snorted. "Yeah. Brilliant."

§

Mel pan-grills the steaks while Ma naps in her recliner. The potatoes bake in the oven, along with three loaves of homemade bread and a small pan of clover-leaf rolls. Mel had come home to the smell of fresh yeasty dough rising in pans on the counter.

Ma had prepared asparagus, too, roasting with garlic, and a salad, tossed and ready in the fridge.

The table is set, with the fancy china and wine glasses; Mel had stopped at the ABC store on the outskirts of Tappahannock on her way home, picking up a six pack of hard cider and a mid-priced merlot to go with the beef. The bottle is chilling in the fridge, next to the salad.

Mel isn't sure her mother will share it with her. It is amazing, as she flips the steaks, how much she doesn't know about her mother. She always thought she knew her mother--and her father--but that relationship isn't as certain as she'd always assumed.

After all, she'd known her mother her whole life. She'd known her father, too, and yet, she'd never known he'd served.

And that bit about possible siblings overseas? She's still reeling from that.

"You okay?"

Mel jumps at the stove, dropping the metal tongs so that they clang to the floor.

"Sorry." Ma steps into the kitchen. "I woke up and smelled dinner on. You looked so far away."

"Just thinking."

"Need help?"

"No." Mel rinses the tongs under the hot water tap and checks the steaks. "I think I'm almost done. You drink wine?"

Ma blinks. "Wine?"

"Yeah, I picked up a bottle to go with the steaks. When I got home, I realized I've never seen you drink and..." Mel shrugs, picking up the pan and plating the steaks.

"I don't usually, but I'll take a little." Ma opens the oven and takes in a deep breath. "I love the scent fresh bread."

Mel laughs. "Me, too. I missed it when I moved out."

The rack squeals when Ma pulls it out and picks up the loaf tins, setting them out to cool. The potatoes come out next, then the roasted asparagus. "Mmm. This all smells good."

"Thanks." Mel grabs the salad and dressing from the fridge, as well as the chilled bottle. "Do you have a cork screw?"

Ma stares at the bottle, eyes wide. After a moment, she shakes her head. "Never needed one."

"S'okay. I know a trick." Mel sets the bottle and salad on the table. "Start eating. I'll be right back."

What she needs she finds in the mudroom: a nail and a hammer. Mel heads back to the kitchen, holding up her tools. She taps the nail into the cork, getting it in good, then wedges the claw under the nail and pulls. She grins when the satisfying pop echoes. "There were no cork screws in Afghanistan, either."

Ma laughs, but stares at Mel a moment too long before holding out her glass. "Then let's be thankful for that."

§

The mess hut was dark and quiet. Mel had been on mess duty earlier and left the latch open when she'd pretended to lock up. She didn't need a light, or the small flashlight she'd brought just in case. The moon lit the floor, and it was a straightaway to the fridge, where she's stashed the bottle of burgundy that hadn't been put in the Colonel's beef stew.

Light from the fridge flooded the room when she opened the door, blinding her. She reached in, found the cold neck of the tall bottle, and pulled it out, closing the door. The darkness returned and she waited while her eyes adjusted.

She waited for her heart beat to slow down, too. If she got caught, she'd be in the Brig for sure.

Leaving, she let the latch fall, truly locking the mess this time. The morning crew would never realize the latch hadn't been down all night.

The motor pool was dark; the ammo hut was dark; the working dog kennels were quiet and dark. She passed them all, walking far away from the barracks, stopping only when her path was blocked by fence.

Near the interior fence, where the pallets were stacked when supplies were unpacked, was also quiet and dark. No one worried about the pallets; they were trash wood. They weren't even sent back to hold more supplies.

The stacks towered over her, not so neat at the top. But they acted as an effective wall, and Mel settled on the ground between two makeshift walls. She unhooked the small hammer in her belt loop and tugged a rusty nail from the nearest pallet.

Using the nail as a corkscrew, she uncorked the bottle, listening after the resounding pop to make sure no one else had heard it and decided to investigate.

The bubbles tickled her tongue and nose. It was earthy and sharp, and hit her empty stomach like a freight train.

Her head swam and she took another long swig. She wanted a buzz, a good high to forget the lousy four days she'd just suffered through. Gunney was a bastard when dumped. Why couldn't he just get some from one of the other girls he'd been fucking? Why was he so pissed that he couldn't fuck her anymore?

She couldn't complain up the chain. Their relationship had been wrong, and she'd be in trouble as much as him. Well, not as much as him, but her career would still be down the shitter.

Another long drink and her thoughts were dancing out of her reach. It was working. She kept drinking, raising the bottle when the wine was done.

Damn. She wanted more.

There was another bottle in the mess.

Forgetting that she'd ensured the latch had made, Mel staggered to her feet, tumbling into a pallet tower, making it teeter. She'd go find another bottle and keep drinking.

The top two pallets tottered off, crashing into another pile, making it shift into the next, which fell against the fence.

"Hey! Who's there?"

*Shit.*

"Manley." The words slurred, and Mel wondered who had answered for her.

Two Marines, one with a rifle at the ready and aimed in her general direction, the other with a flashlight pointed in her face, rounded the wobbley wall.

"Hey!" Mel raised the bottle to shade her face.

"Are you drunk?" The one with the flashlight stepped forward and snatched the bottle from her hand. "Where did you get this?"

Mel shrugged and flopped back to the ground. Closing her eyes, she snorted and rubbed her hands over her eyes. "Want my bed."

"I bet you do." The glare vanished and a strong arm wound around her torso, a hand grabbing her arm to drape it over his shoulder. "Let's get you there, then okay? Can you walk?"

"Sure." The word rolled off her tongue and fell to the ground. "I can dance, too."

"Well, we just need you to walk, Sergeant."

Mel turned her head to look at the Marine holding her up, and the world tilted and twirled. "Ooh."

"Okay?" The Marine led her out of the towers of pallets, the second watchman following, his gun now lowered but still ready.

"Mhmm." Mel moved her feet. They felt light and floaty and she had a little trouble finding the ground.

"Don't barf on me, okay? I only got one other clean uniform right now and I need it for tomorrow."

**8**

· ✦ ·

## MEMORIES

"Y our Dad used to get that look on his face, too." Ma sits across the table, her wine glass still almost full. She's taken sips, but that's all.

Mel swirls the liquid in her own goblet. It is her third glass, and there is heat in her cheeks. "Just thinking."

"About Afghanistan?"

"About a man. In Afghanistan." Mel laughs and takes a long sip of wine.

"You care about him?"

"I did. I don't anymore. He came home and, well, I guess we don't know each other anymore. But-" Mel chokes on her words. How can she talk about her relationship with Gunney to her mother? "He was a mistake."

"A mistake?" Her mother sets her glass on the table and rises. "Keep talking; I'll fetch dessert."

Dessert was more cake with whipped cream and gingered peaches her mother had canned last year. It was sweet and spicy and creamy—a lot of different tastes that work well together.

Mel wishes for white wine to go with it. A sweet white to compliment the peaches and clean the palate after the spice.

"Mel?"

"He was married. I knew it. But he said the marriage was on the rocks. She couldn't handle him being in the service." Mel licked the tines of her fork. She couldn't look at her mother.

"Were they divorcing?"

"She wanted one. I think she started the paperwork." Mel's voice roughens and she clears her throat, but whatever is blocks her windpipe doesn't move. "I don't know what happened when he got back stateside."

"And?"

"I wasn't the only one. I only figured it out after... I ended things once I found out."

Ma is silent a moment. "Your Dad had women in Vietnam. I think, for some, it helps them cope with what they have to do."

"Maybe. But when I called it off, he wasn't very... nice." Shit. No, nice wasn't even close to how he'd been. "I never imagined he'd be like that. I thought he cared, even if I wasn't the only one."

"Oh, sweetie." Ma reaches across the table, taking her hand and squeezing. "You still care, don't you?"

Yes, but no. Mel still cares, but it's more shame and anger at being used than an emotion about Gunney and the stuff that happened after; stuff she can't talk to her mother about. She couldn't tell her shrink about it. It's not something folks talked about; no one wanted to hear that kind of story, no one believed you when you told it.

Ma swallows hard enough Mel can see her neck muscles contract. Sniffing, Mel looks away. She doesn't want to cry. It isn't worth it. It hurts, and it shouldn't. She knows more about that SOB than him fucking every girl in a skirt and then some.

"Mel? What else is there? I can tell that isn't all." Ma doesn't let go of her hand. "We may have drifted apart, but I will always be your mother."

The tears fall. Mel can't stop them. The lump in her throat grows, making it hard to breathe.

Ma rubs her hand, her thumb stroking over the back. "Okay, you don't have to tell me now."

Nodding, Mel sniffs and blinks. The tears keep falling, tracing down her cheeks and dripping from her chin. They hit the table, a temporary stain on the wood.

Ma stands and gathers the dirty dishes, piling them at the sink. "How about we watch a movie? Brad and Chrissie got me a Blue Ray player at Christmas and I have a small collection of romantic comedies. Do you like Sandra Bullock?"

"Who doesn't?" Mel pushes the words out and swipes a hand over her face. She downs the last of her wine and considers what's left in the bottle.

"I can put it in a stew tomorrow." Ma stands, wiping wet hands on a towel.

Mel nods and rams the cork back in the neck. "Good idea."

"Go grab a chair and I'll be right in."

Stumbling out of her chair, Mel rights herself at the corner of the table. "Sorry about that."

"It's okay, Mel. It's probably as much the emotion as the wine. Or it's your leg." Ma watches her face, like she's looking for a sign, maybe confirmation, information.

There it is. Mel waits a moment before sighing. "I got bit. Bad. The kid that did the tourniquet saved my life, but made it too tight and it took my leg."

"Oh." Ma stands, hands clasped, staring like she can see the prosthetic below the fabric of Mel's pant leg.

Mel would love to think her mother is right, that it's emotion and her leg, but it isn't. The already-empty bottle of merlot in the trash bin outside, emptied while she sat in the truck at the end of the driveway, is testament to just how much of this is due to alcohol.

She thought being here would help her stop. But it hasn't. It isn't making it worse, though. The six pack is still full and waiting. Waiting, but not calling to her.

"I'm going to go sit." Mel straightens and limps to the living room. Her mother knows it's there; there's no reason to rub the skin raw pretending otherwise. She stops at the edge of the kitchen. "Okay if I take it off when I sit down?"

"Yeah, sure." Ma has half the dishes in the washer, and the food nearly put away.

A twinge of guilt makes Mel take a step to help, but the pinch on her leg is stronger, and she turns back toward the den and relief.

The chairs, both recliners, are set at angles in the center of the room, each with a straight view to the new TV. Though identical when purchased, the seat of one is concave, though not much, the circular dip a little lighter than the rest of the chair.

Mel chooses the newer-looking recliner. It is her Dad's and smells like her memories of him, like his cigars and Old Spice. Once seated, she rolls up her pant leg and rips off the Velcro that holds the limb to her knee. The skin is red and, sure enough, the cotton and padding in the cup is tinged pink. She'll have to clean it carefully before bed and wrap it lightly in gauze. Pulling the folded fabric down to cover the stub, she pushes herself back in the chair and stows the prosthetic, out of the line of sight of the other chair.

Ma chooses a thin sleeve from a shelf and takes the disc out, slipping it into the player on a shelf below the TV and pressing the play button. The TV turns on, the blue glow brightening to show the opening screen.

When the movie starts, Mel relaxes back into the recliner, letting the music run through her. She knows the movie, knows the jokes and humor, the antics and melodrama, but it doesn't matter. It is something to enjoy with her mother, to take charge of her brain and, at least for the moment, overwrite the intruding memories of Gunney.

§

It was movie night every Friday in the mess hall, with popcorn and nachos. Everyone had to sit at a table, watching the film with necks twisted, and Mel always ended up with a crick and a bad night's sleep.

They could drink beer on Fridays, too, if they still had a beer chit. It was doubled though, so a chit for one bottle meant you could have two.

Most of the Marines and Soldiers could handle two beers, but there were ways to get more than the two, even if you only had one chit left. You could buy a chit for ten bucks, more if chits were scarce. That sometimes happened in a five Friday month.

Chits were handed out on a per-month basis, and those fifth Fridays meant four weeks of beer night had passed. If you were smart, you held out for that fifth Friday; chits were worth twenty-five a pop on those rare days, and Marines who needed more would pay up.

While Mel liked a beer, it wasn't her favorite libation, and she had connections to get what she liked. And she wasn't naive enough to drink in a crowd.

So, her chits were up for sale more often than not. But you had to be careful. Though everyone knew it happened, it wasn't an approved procedure by any means, and getting caught was an offense punishable by mess duty and a loss of beer chits for the following month.

Gunney always bought chits, and Mel had no problem giving hers over, money or not. At least, she did before the fight.

That first Friday after was messy. He wanted her chits, but she didn't want to give them to him. Not for free, not for money, not for a lot of money and an easy watch duty.

He got mad and ranted through the movie, enough that he got kicked out.

Mel felt uneasy after the movie. She couldn't remember what they'd watched, or who had sat at her table and used her beer chits. She'd walked back to her Quonset barrack tense, the usual neck crick stiffening her spine and into her shoulders.

The hair on her nape rose.

Gunney was waiting. Even without her chits, he was drunk. He grabbed her and pulled her behind him. Mel didn't want to yell. She didn't want to make more trouble for Gunney. She could talk to him.

But she couldn't. Not that night, anyway.

She hadn't wanted to, but he hadn't listened. He'd ignored her protest, her 'no's and 'please stop's and 'you're hurting me's'. When he was done, spent and breathing heavy but steady, on the verge of sleep, Mel had been able to push him off and pull her pants back on. She'd staggered back to the barrack hut—not sure where she was, where she was going, but not really lost—crawled into a hot shower and sobbed under the running water.

All she wanted, in that moment, was to go home. To crawl into the bed in her teenage bedroom and forget everything about Gunney, the Marines, Afghanistan. That night. *Everything*.

But she couldn't. Reveille came at the usual time, though she hadn't been able to sleep. She rose, took another shower—cold this time—and ate a quick breakfast or cereal and lukewarm milk. She didn't talk to anyone, but grabbed her tools and got to work changing the oil in her assigned HUMVEE.

No one spoke to her, either, seeming to understand something had happened last night and she was just plain pissed off.

All had been good until just before lunch, when everyone was called into the mess. The lines were closed, the mess specialists still prepping and cooking food. They were called out, too, and Mel suspected that lunch would be served late.

She didn't care; she wasn't hungry. Though for once, she actually wanted a beer.

LtCol stood in front of the still hanging movie screen, pale and sweaty. He swallowed, and removed his cover to ruffle the scant hair on his head. "I've called you all here to give you some bad news. The caravan due to arrive this morning was attacked by insurgents. We're locking down the base until further notice. Casualties were taken back to the main Garrison at Helmand."

Mel stared. She'd been in an attack before, but not with casualties. She knew the bullets were real, but this was too close to home. She could have been in that caravan. She knew people who were. Had one of her friends been killed?

Murmurs spread through the Marines, the surge of voices rising, louder and louder, echoing in the small space. Bodies shifted on the benches, sitting squeezed enough together so that clothing rustled.

Names were whispered. Some she knew, had driven with, stood watch with. Some she only recognized the name from the duty roster or watch call.

"Fall out. Get back to work. Be on alert." The LtCol called out, his voice dropping over the whispers but not stopping them. He walked out, shoulders slumped, sweat stains dark at his armpits and lower back.

For Mel, what had happened last night shrank into nothing, just a small blip in a larger dark spreading mass. She shut it away, going back to the motor pool and her torn-apart HUMVEE and tools.

# 9

## SET AFLAME

Mel isn't happy to be stranded in front of the fire department.

Ozzie is a firefighter, though the whole unit is mostly volunteer. So, he might not be at the station right now.

"Hey, Mel. Truck break down?"

Yeah, right; her luck had left her long ago. It has to be *Ozzie*.

Plastering a smile on stiff lips, Mel turns to her old friend, focusing on his neck. "Yeah. I think it's the carburetor. Not sure when Ma had it serviced last."

Ozzie laughs, throwing his head back. "Not surprised. I think your Dad took care of that stuff."

"Figures. They had a very traditional marriage. I'm not sure he knew how to boil water. The kitchen was her domain." Damn. She's blabbering about nothing when all she really wants is for him to leave.

"Do you want me to take a look?"

"No, I checked and I'm pretty sure it's the carburetor." Mel stiffens, waiting for him to insist on checking. Most men do. It drives her nuts; she was a damn good mechanic in the Marines. Still is a damn good mechanic; she hadn't left her know-how behind.

"Okay." Ozzie nods, cocking his head to look at her sideways. "Want me to call Sheldon for a tow?"

"Sheldon still runs the tow truck?" Last she remembers, Sheldon is 90 already.

"Sheldon the fourth, it is now. His, what, great-grand-son, I think." Frowning, Ozzie looks off in to the distance. "Or was old Sheldon a junior and this one is fifth?"

Mel laughs. She can't help it. Ozzie could always make anyone laugh. That was why she had such a crush on him in high school. A hard enough crush that her heart skips when he turns back to grin at her. "Yeah. Better call him. It's not going anywhere on its own."

God, she just needs to stay away from men who can make her laugh.

Ozzie waves for her to follow him, and she does, straining to keep her eyes on his broad shoulders and not on his well-formed butt. She sighs.

"You okay?" At the door, he looks back at her, pushing it in and pausing in the threshold.

"Yeah. Just tired." Her limp is back

"I'm still waiting for you to run with me."

Mel's stomach swoops. He means going for a run, down the road, in sneakers and sweats, but a small part of her wishes he meant otherwise. "Give me another week." She would have to see about asking her VA doctor about running with the athletic prosthetic. *If* he'd talk to her.

"Okay. Remember, I'm only getting faster." Ozzie grabs up the receiver and punches in a number by heart. The ringing on the other end is loud enough that Mel can hear it. No one answers, and the answering machine message is garbled. "Hey, Sheldon, this is Ozzie at the station. Mel's truck broke down and needs a tow over to the shop. Give me a call on my cell when you're available."

Ozzie shrugs. "Best I can do. I could call all the way to Richmond, but it would be tomorrow before they could send anyone out.

"S'okay. I need to talk to Gary at the shop—it is still Gary right?" At Ozzie's smirk and nod, she continues, "—and then find a ride back to the farm."

"Well then, aren't I lucky? And you, too. I was in to check the equipment and the two kids working the full Saturday shift, so I can run you by the shop and then to the farm on my way home. Just give me a sec to sign the log." Ozzie disappears into the back, leaving Mel to wait.

And she does. She's not a hundred percent sure why. Anyone could drive her to the shop. Hell, she could walk there in less than half an hour. But she waits. It's Ozzie. She sighs and looks over the photos on the wall. Some are old, of the first volunteer force the town had, a handwritten 1917 written in blue ink on one corner. Others are new, and she sees Ozzie standing tall in the back row of the last three.

"Ready?" Ozzie grabs a jacket and slings it over his arm.

Mel nods and follows him out the door, which he locks behind them. "The farm isn't on the way to your house?"

He glances her way and shrugs. "I don't live with my parents. I'm staying with Charlie until things get settled."

"Things?" Mel stomach jumps at the possibility. "Settled?"

Ozzie snorts. "I forgot you don't know."

"Hmm?" She tries not to sound too interested.

"Joanie and I are separated, have been for a while, and I finally decided it was time to file for a divorce. My mum has the kids, has had them for a while actually."

*Divorce.*

Ozzie swallows and looks at the sky, like he's looking for answers. "Joanie and I got complicated and it was better for Lexie and Barry. My mother stepped in to help while Joanie and I worked on being a couple again, but that," he sucks in a breath, "well, we aren't ever going to be a couple again. I finally accepted that."

"Oh. Sorry things didn't work out." *Right. Lie like you mean it.*

Shrugging again, he stares a moment. "Anyway. My car is parked out back." He nods toward the dirt path that runs along the edge of the lawn, between the fire station truck bay and the fence that runs the perimeter of the elementary school.

They are quiet walking to the car, and getting into the car, and while Ozzie drives. At the garage, Mel hops out and jogs inside, ignoring the pinch on her knee; she doesn't want Ozzie asking questions about a limp. Gary's daughter, Delta-Dawn—named after the song, of course—sits behind a raised counter.

"Hey, Mel. Heard you were back in town." Delta is a couple years younger than Mel, but Gary is older than Mel's Dad would have been. She's a late baby, born after the rest of the brood were already in high school.

"Yeah. Visiting Ma." Mel leans on the counter. "Look, the truck broke down by the fire station, and I've got a call in to Sheldon to tow it over here. It's the carburetor, and I was wondering if I left you the keys, if Gary could fix it. Not a rush, just whenever he has the time."

"Sure." Delta picks up a clip board and writes on it, holding out her hand for the keys. Mel drops them into the palm. "He probably won't get a chance to start on it until tomorrow. You got a way home?"

"Ozzie's dropping me off. And I have my car to drive around in until it's working, so there isn't a rush."

"Yum. Ozzie." Delta smiles like she knows something and Mel looks out the dusty window. Ozzie is sitting in the car, tapping the steering wheel with his fingers. He must be listening to the radio. "I can't wait until his divorce is through."

"Oh? You two an item?"

Delta snorts. "Heck, no. Ozzie don't play that way. Not now anyway. But once he's available, I plan to make a run on him. I'll need to be quick, though. Half of Tappahannock's women are waiting for it to happen. Probably a good portion of the women in Richmond, too."

Mel signs the work form when it's offered and nods. "Okay. Do you need a credit card number?"

Waving, Delta pins the form to the corkboard behind her. "We'll get it when it's done. We know your family." She slides a glance at Mel. "You've been in the big city too long. You've forgotten how it works here."

Laughing, Mel lies and agrees with her. Big city indeed. "I should try to come back more often."

"Why not move back?" Delta leans on her side of the counter. "You got somebody in the city?"

"What?" Mel rears back and shakes her head. "No."

"Cool. Look, the Red Wagon has a girls' night on third Friday—and that's this Friday. Cheap beer. Scantily clad male dancers. Why don't you come out?"

"Not sure it's my thing." It didn't sound like fun to Mel.

"Well, we all meet up and have fun. Wynne doesn't let guys in the door—except Paul and Shaeffer, cause, well, they're a guy couple, so it's okay. She makes them sit in the back, so the dancers aren't freaked out."

Mel can't help the snicker. "We'll see."

"Okay. I'll call you when I know something about the truck."

"Thanks."

The little bell above the door jingles on her way out and Ozzie, sitting with the window open, grins and leans out. "What were you doing, explaining how to swap out the carburetor?"

"No. Just doing a little catching up." No way is she telling Ozzie about Delta's plans for him, even if she doesn't agree—especially because she doesn't agree. "And she invited me to girls' night at the Red Wagon."

"Ah. Joanie likes going to that. I think the whole womenfolk show up for third Fridays."

Mel tugs the handle of her door and it sticks, so Ozzie has to lean over and open it from the inside. "Sorry, that door isn't used much."

Sliding in, pausing, lifting her left leg higher to pull it in, Mel considers a possible conversation. "How far do you run?" She rubs over the knee, above the tight Velcro band.

"Huh?" Frowning at her hand, Ozzie already has the car in gear, but puts it back in park to gape.

"You want me to go for a run with you. How far do you plan on us running?"

"However far you want." His frown deepens and he shoots a glance to her knee. "Uh, Mel, can you run?"

She stills her fingers, realizing what she's been doing. Looking down at her knee, she shrugs. "To be honest, i'm not sure."

He glances down to where she;s still rubbing her knee. "You got hurt over there?"

Mel bunches her pant leg in her fingers and pulls it up, displaying the usually hidden prosthetic. She waits for the gasp, the oh-no-you-poor-thing, the stiffening in the seat.

Ozzie snorts. "You were going to run on that?"

Blinking, Mel faces him and snorts back. "No. I have an athletic one, too. But I haven't used it except walking on a treadmill and using an elliptical. And that was under a therapist's watch. That's why I'm asking about how far you want to run."

"How about we start with a mile or two and see how we do?" Ozzie shakes his head at her. "So, is your other one built for running?"

"Built for athletic pursuits." Mel snickers. "This one is built for a man. I need to buy shoes with odd sizes so I can wear a matching pair."

"What?" He twists in his seat. "You mean they don't have 'em in women's sizes?"

Mel sighs. At least he's not lecturing on how she shouldn't have been over there anyway. "I guess they buy in bulk." It's supposed to be a joke, a dark one, but it's supposed to make you laugh and ease the tension.

"That's just fucked up."

They stare into each other's eyes a full minute before Ozzie pulls his gaze away and Mel drops hers back to the knee, resuming the massage.

The car jerks when Ozzie puts it back into reverse. "Damn, we may be running to the farm. I'll have to drop this off to get looked at soon." He backs the car out and it jerks again when he puts it in drive.

"Do you want me to push?"

"What?" Ozzie shoots her a look.

"The car."

"No, I think it'll be fine going forward."

"You sure? I can take a look at it if you want." Mel rolls down her window—it's manual—and folds her elbow on top, stretching the prosthesis as straight as she can.

Ozzie shakes his head. "That may not go back up."

Mel raises a brow.

"And you can take that off if you need to."

Shaking her head, Mel watches out the window. "It's fine." But she's grinning, her insides humming with the realization that he doesn't care that she's missing a piece.

§

There were bullet holes in the side, some dents, and a missing side mirror.

Mel stared at the transport vehicle. It had been full of Soldiers when it had been shot at, and a couple got hit, but were going to live. The casualties had been in the ammo truck when it blew up.

She pulled the hood release and pushed the heavy metal panel up, standing on tip-toe to lift it high enough for it to catch and hold. It had been hit in the radiator, too, and fluid streamed all over the engine.

"I'm gonna need a new radiator." Mel tapped the hoses, checking connections. She couldn't think about the Soldiers; just the truck. The truck was just a truck—she could fix it.

And if it couldn't be fixed, it would be used for parts to fix another one.

"I'll go grab the one off the skeleton."

The skeleton was parked out back--there were three in reality—none fixable, all kept to donate parts for those that could be repaired. One was down to its frame, only a fender and a door remaining from the body.

"What's taking you so long?" The Staff Sergeant growled from the open bay doors.

"It just came in." Mel's head was buried in the engine compartment. She was trying to track down a dripping leak, but couldn't identify the liquid yet; it had mixed with the radiator fluid, and had a sheen that wasn't oil or transmission fluid.

"I don't want excuses, Manley."

"Not an excuse, a fact." Mel pulled her head up and frowned at the fluid on her fingers, rubbing her thumb through it to test for grit. She couldn't feel any, so it likely wasn't oil. It must be trans fluid.

"Watch it Manley." The SSgt marched into his office.

"Yeah." Mel opened the trans fluid reservoir; it was empty. The SSgt always gave her a hard time, so she'd learned to not react. It made the tirades shorter.

"Here you go." The Private handed her a radiator. It was dented but whole.

"Thanks. Set it down right there." Mel pointed in front of the truck. Do we have transmission fluid in the bay, or do I have to go over to supply?"

"Probably at supply. I'll go get it for you." The kid grinned.

"No, don't do that." Mel wiped her hands on a towel. She glanced toward the office where the SSgt sat behind his desk with his feet up. "We don't need any trouble. I'll go fetch it once I figure out what needs to be replaced in the trans line."

"You sure?" The Private leaned over the side of the truck, poking at the radiator hose. "It's nothing for me to go get it for you."

"I know, but remember what happened last time."

Last time, Mel had gotten reamed into a strip for enticing the Private into doing her work for her. All the kid had done was hold a part in place while Mel screwed it in, but the SSgt had been convinced she'd done something inappropriate.

Gunney had heard and bullied the Staff Sergeant, but that hadn't fixed anything, only made it worse.

"Private, don't you have something better to do than jabber at her? She needs to get that truck moving again." The SSgt poked his head out of his office. "I need office supplies; here's a list."

The kid took the piece of paper and trudged out the door, mouthing a 'sorry' when he passed Mel.

Mel ignored him. Ignored the Staff Sergeant. She'd found the torn transmission line. Jumping down from the stool she used to access the engine, she brushed her hands on her overalls and grabbed her tool bag. She needed a donor hose.

"Where you going?"

"Out to the skeleton." She left, not looking back. She knew one thing, the Staff Sergeant wouldn't touch the truck. He wasn't that stupid. Though he gave her a hard time—and the Private whenever he spoke to her—she knew her job and did it well.

"Hey, Mel." Gunney waved and jogged over. "Whatcha doing tonight?"

"Sleeping." She yanked open the gate that led to the graveyard and marched through. The truck needed to be fixed before chow.

"I mean before that." Gunney followed through the gate, throwing an arm over her shoulder, squeezing her close to her side. "I mean something you and I could do together."

Mel insides turned to mush and smiled at him. "What time?"

"After chow. You be at early dinner?" Gunney scouted for spies and nuzzled her neck.

Shying away from the tickle, Mel giggled and pushed him away when he went for more. "I'll do my best. But I need to fix this truck first."

Gunney licked her neck and pulled her closer, one hand clasping over her right buttock.

"Gunney." Mel hissed and pushed harder. "Someone could see."

"Jeez, Mel. What's wrong with you?"

"I have a truck to fix. The Staff Sergeant is already on my case." She threw his arm off and marched to the skeleton that still had an engine, digging through the cavity to see if the transmission line was still in one piece. It was.

"Five minutes won't matter."

Mel snorted. "It wouldn't just be five minutes, and you know it."

"I can't help it if I'm that good." Gunney swaggered and wagged his brows.

"I have a job, Gunney. Let me do it, okay."

He sighed and spun around. "Fine. I'll see you after chow, if I'm not busy."

Mel shook her head and pulled the usable hose from the skeleton. At least she had something to look forward to later. Tucking the hose into the bag, she trudged back to the garage.

"Was that Gunney Myers?" A Staff Sergeant—another mechanic, but a supervisor—met her at the open bay door.

Aw, hell. "Yeah."

"You got lockup duty." He smirked and retreated to the office.

"Fuck." Mel walked to the truck and stepped on the stool, yanking the broken hose out. No way was she making early chow now.

"Sorry about that. I tried to keep him inside." The Private stood at the edge of the engine compartment, a box of office supplies in his arms.

"S'okay kid." But it wasn't, not really. Gunney would not be happy when she didn't show.

# 10

## RUNNING

At the farm, watching the spiraling dust cloud that follows Ozzie's junker, Mel realizes he still hadn't told her when they'd be running. It didn't matter. She'd just wanted to talk about something, and she'd figured the run was an easy topic, and they'd have set a time and date for it.

She's unsure why she wants a date; she doesn't *want* to run with him, does she?

If he's in the midst of divorcing Joanie, maybe it was time to scratch that itch. Just once. Just to get some relief.

"Mel? Is that you?" Ma rounds the end of the house.

"Yeah, it's me. The truck broke down, so Ozzie drove me home."

"Where's the truck? At Gary's?"

"Not yet." Mel saunters toward her mother, her mind only half on the conversation at hand. She takes short steps, so there's no pinch. "Ozzie called Sheldon to tow it but had to leave a message."

"A message?" Ma frowns.

"Yeah. No one picked up the phone."

"Okay."

"We stopped at Gary's shop, so he knows it's coming and has the keys." Mel takes a deep breath once she's in the back door. The house smells like sugar and ginger. "What are you making?"

"Gingerbread. I thought we could have it for dessert with dinner." Ma stares at Mel.

"What?" Mel raises her brows and her voice.

"Nothing." Ma shrugs and turns away.

Mel sighs. "Ma." Her mother has that hard-thinking look on her face. The one she always gets when something didn't make sense or add up. She always got that look on her face when Mel told a lie to cover up doing something she wasn't supposed to have done.

"I said nothing. I wonder what's wrong with the truck." Ma steps up to the stove and opens the oven, the blast of heated air making it all the way to Mel. She takes out the cake pan filled with hot spicy cake.

Pulling out a chair to sit, Mel runs her hand through her hair. "It's the carburetor."

"Oh. Is that what Ozzie said?"

"Ozzie didn't look at it. I did. It's the carburetor." Mel shoves her chair back, the legs scraping on the floor. "I'm going for a walk, okay?"

She doesn't want to be mad at her mother. Ma has no idea what she did in the Marines. Maybe that's what makes her mad the most, that her mother doesn't know. And has never bothered to ask. Being a Marine was more than carrying a gun and shooting at people.

Outside, the breeze is cool on her heated cheeks, and she stalks toward the creek, the pinching back, stopping when she catches sight of a tall figure walking up the dirt drive. "I thought you said it would be fine going forward?"

Ozzie waves and speeds to a jog, yelling so  the words reach her. "I guess I was wrong."

"Need a ride?"

He shrugs, stopping his jog when he reaches her. "Or a phone. I can call Charlie. He can pick me up on his way home after work."

"Oswald Kirby! I haven't seen you since the baptism." Once again, Ma rounds the corner of the house, this time with a dish towel in her hands. "I hear you left a message for Sheldon to tow the truck."

Flushing, Ozzie looks away. "Yes ma'am."

"Good. Have you had dinner?"

He licks his lips and glances to Mel, who's looking from him to her mother, frowning.

"Um. No, ma'am."

"Good for that, too. I've got meatloaf and mashed potatoes and veggies. Probably too much and we won't be able to eat it all." Ma turns and heads back into the house. "I'll set the table and call you in when it's all ready."

"What's up with leaving a message for Sheldon?"

"Nothing." Ozzie rattles the change in his pocket.

"Ozzie. Don't lie to me. I can, and will, kick your ass. This prosthesis is heavy resin and metal. It will hurt you."

"Yeah, I know. Look, Sheldon doesn't always check his messages. But don't worry, Gary will call him if he doesn't show up with the truck. I was going to call when I got home, but-" He shrugs.

Mel sighs. "Sometimes I forget what it's like living here."

"What do you mean?"

She takes a deep breath. "The air is clear, and the food is great, but my cell gets no signal, not even in town. And girls' night is only one day a month. And there's a limited number of eligible men so when one's available, it's like a cat fight to get his attention." Shit. Why had she added that last?

"You looking for an eligible man?"

"Well, no." But isn't she?

"Sure? Because right here soon, I'm going to be eligible." Ozzie's gaze is intense.

Mel isn't sure how to respond to that. It sounds like Ozzie is interested—in her. "Delta says you don't play that way." She feels the heat rise up her neck and flood her face. Oh, God. He'd said when he was eligible. And she'd jumped to-

Fingers—*his fingers*—on her cheek make her thoughts jump the track and disappear into a deep ravine. "I don't play with Delta at all."

His face is close, almost too close; Mel can see the fine hairs on his upper cheek as well as the darker, thicker stubble on his jaw.

"I learned the hard way that playing can get you in trouble."

Mel nods, the movement removing his fingers. Her cheek is chilled with their warmth gone. "Yeah. Me, too."

"Supper's on!" The call comes through the window, the flutter of curtaintelling them Ma has been watching. They turn as one, Ozzie's fingers falling away, leaving Mel missing them.

Ozzie sighs. "Sheldon doesn't have an answering machine. I called and left the message on the mayor's line."

"Why?" Mel rounds on him, hands on her hips. It's easier to be mad at him; it means she doesn't have to examine those other feelings.

"If he'd come and towed the truck, he'd have brought you home. And I wanted to bring you home."

Mel's not sure what to say. So, she says nothing and stares at his jaw. He's clenching it so the muscle below his ear bulges.

"He's one of those eligible guys you're looking for." Ozzie shoves his hands in his jacket pockets and shuffles toward the house.

"I said I wasn't looking."

"Hard not to look at him."

She raises her brows. She remembers Sheldon whatever-the-number from high school. He hung around with her brother when sober. "Really? Not the way I remember him. And besides, he'll probably wind up looking like old Sheldon." She shudders for emphasis.

"Well, you remember wrong then. He's the *numero uno* bachelor in town." They're at the back door and Ma is humming in the kitchen.

"The way I hear, there's a line forming to make you the new number one when you hit eligibility." Mel points to his jacket so she can hang it on a hook.

He shrugs out of it. "Really? I hadn't heard."

"Then you need to listen better." The jacket looks like it belongs on the hook, hanging next to hers, and Mel wonders what's gotten into her.

"Maybe." But he doesn't sound like he believes it. "Hey, Mrs. Manley? Can I borrow your phone?"

"I can drive you home." Mel stares. Has she pissed him off? She doesn't want to.

He smirks. "I need to call Sheldon, or your truck will still be sitting next to the fire station in the morning."

"Oh."

"Of course, you can, Ozzie. You know where it is, right?"

"Yes, ma'am."

**11**

# SPEEDY COMPACT

The Miata is too small for Ozzie. His knees jam up into the dash and he slouches so his head isn't smashed into the headliner.

"Sorry." She stares at his pretzeled length. "You can put the seat back."

"S'okay. It's your car, not mine. I like that it runs without jerking our internal organs into mush." He fumbles for the lever on the bottom on the seat and it slowly moves back, letting him unfold like a broken slinky in slow motion.

Mel laughs. "I hadn't thought about how tall you are when I insisted on driving you home. I guess I should have asked Ma for the keys to her Impala."

They're on the road, heading back into town. It's dusk and Mel hunts for the sign that tells her where to turn for Charlie's place.

"There." Ozzie points and Mel turns, the car making a clean swooping arc even on the dirt. "This car does drive easy."

"I like it." Mel glances at Ozzie's knees, still touching the glove compartment door. "I know that can't be comfortable, though."

He shrugs. "It's better than walking."

"Are you sure?"

"That's my story."

The Miata is the only car on the road, which is paved, so the ride is smoother.

"The next drive on the right. He has a trout carving on the top of the mailbox." Ozzie points ahead, though Mel can't see anything yet.

Her headlights sweep ahead of them, lighting up the bright green twisting fish atop a matte black box.

She slows and turns in, the headlights flashing over a two-story log cabin with attached garage. "Nice."

"Yeah. Charlie built it himself a couple years ago. I helped with the deck out back last summer when he said I could stay with him instead of trying to rent somewhere in town." Ozzie unkinks his frame, stretching both arms and legs once he's outside the car.

"Handy talent to have around."

"He's gay."

"I thought only Paul and Schaeffer were gay."

"No, they're gay, and a couple, and like to watch straight men prance around taking their clothes off for women while drinking virgin pina coladas."

"Virgin pina coladas? What's the point in that?"

"To stay sober. If they get hammered—which they did the first time Wynne let them in—they make passes at the dancers, who don't appreciate it, and punch them bloody."

"Ooh. Yeah. I think I'd stick to virgin pina coladas after that, too."

"Want a beer? We can sit out on the deck. It'll give you a chance to admire my handy talents."

"Sure, but just one. I need to drive back."

§

"Beer's not my thing." Mel curled her lip at the bottle Gunney held for her.

"Look, it's all I got." The older Marine pushed the alcoholic offering closer to her face.

Mel could smell the hops; she'd rather have cider, but take the bottle with a half-hearted smile. "Okay, thanks."

They clink bottles and Gunney takes a long swig, clearing half the liquid in his in one go. He smacks his lips and scratches a hairy bare leg. They'd been on a long drill run with a couple other Marines, running in circles inside the inside perimeter fence of the base. Saturdays were reserved for drilling and running and all the regular stuff Marines did to stay ready for anything.

Next Saturday was a mock CFT.

The beer was cold and felt good going down her throat, if not on her tongue. Mel took another swallow. The second wasn't as bad as the first.

The other runners also had beers, sitting on the dusty ground, dark olive-green t-shirts and shorts wet with sweat.

"So, Manley. Where you from?" Gunney finishes his bottle off and picks another one out of the white cooler.

"Virginia."

"That's a big state. Wanna be more specific?" Gunney chugged his second beer and fished for his third.

Mel watched, wary, sipping her own drink. One of the other runners finished his first and went for his second. "Where'd the beer come from?" Bottles filled the cooler--a lot of chits.

"Someone messed up and no one got chits last night. So, I appropriated the spoils." Gunney grinned and held up his beer in a toast-like fashion.

The other runners held theirs up, too, and laughed. There were about a dozen of them in total; Mel was the new kid on the block. And the only female.

"My parents live in a little town outside Tappahannock." Mel did her best to not smile.

"Where the fuck is that?"

She smirked. "About an hour from Richmond, on the Rappahannock River. They own a small farm."

"Your dad's a farmer?" The question came from one of the other runners, a tall lanky kid with freckles and what might be red hair. "Mine grows corn in Ohio."

The sergeant next to him jabs an elbow into the kid's side. "Ohio's a big state. Wanna be more specific?"

The group laughs and Mel wonders if she's missed the joke, or if it's just the beer giggling.

"Akron is the biggest town any of you dicks would recognize." The kid shook his head and took a drink. Mel didn't think he looked old enough to be legal.

"Hey," Gunney waved a hand, "be nice. We have a guest." He pointed to Mel.

"I'm a guest?" Mel stared hard at Gunney. "Because I'm a girl?"

"Because you're new to Afghanistan."

"It's not like I'm leaving tomorrow." Mel finished the last of her beer all at once, and it rushed her head.

A dark-haired Marine stood and stretched. "Some do." He dropped his empty bottle back in the cooler and sauntered off.

Mel blinked, not sure what he meant.

The red head shrugged, seeming to notice her confusion. "Some don't make it. Others, well, they get an ear with the Colonel and then go home."

Standing, Mel set her empty in the cooler with the others and considered if she wanted a second. She'd only been here a week, but it wasn't her first OCONUS duty station. She knew the game.

And another drink was a bad move.

"I don't plan to go home early." Nodding, she walked away, wishing she'd said no to the beer.

§

"Here." Ozzie holds out a familiar brown bottle.

"Thanks." The bottle is cold, condensation coating the outside, making her hand wet. She takes a swig; it tastes clean, but it's not a sweet cider. "I see you don't go for cheap beer."

"Nope. Don't see the sense in it." Ozzie settles in the Adirondack chair next to hers, stretching his legs out in front of him. He sighs and takes a long swig. "If it doesn't taste good, why drink it?"

Mel laughs. "So, the point of drinking isn't to get drunk?"

"Not anymore. Did enough of that when I was younger. Too risky now."

"Risky?" Mel takes another mouthful of brew and settles back in the chair. This is nice, sitting and drinking and talking. No alarms or gunfire or senior officer looking for other people's trouble. No pressure.

Ozzie nods. "Yeah. That's how Joanie got pregnant. That's why we ended up married. I thought that was the only way to handle it."

"Oh. I thought—well, she always said you'd asked."

"Well, yes I did, after I found out she was pregnant. That wasn't in either of our plans, though, and I think we both resented Lexie changing everything. Not that any of it was the baby's fault, but, hell, Joanie and I were still kids, too."

Mel considers what she knows about Joanie. "I'm not sure it was a mistake on her part."

"You mean you think she got pregnant on purpose?" Ozzie's side glance tells her he's already figured that out.

She nods. "Just how she acted after the wedding. I didn't figure it out back then, only now, with what you said." She doesn't want him thinking she'd been keeping something from him.

"I didn't figure it out back then, either. She had to tell me, when she told me she never wanted kids. But she'd wanted me, I guess, and figured if she had me everything else would work out." Ozzie finishes his bottle and stares into its empty depths.

"I'm sorry."

"She also told me that Barry isn't mine, though I suspected that already. She'd been cheating for a while. Me, too, if I'm being honest. Our marriage wasn't much after a couple of years."

Mel stares at Ozzie. What could she say? What did he expect?

"Look, I'm not proud of how I handled myself back then. I was young. So was she, I suppose. I wasn't happy; I was angry. I didn't want to be married." Ozzie sets his bottle on the deck. "I don't think she did, either. Not the way we were married, anyway."

"I thought she wanted it. I mean, the way she talked about it." Mel sloshes the beer around in her bottle, staring at her feet.

"I don't think it met her expectations."

"Expectations?"

"I think she expected to stay home, and I would go to work, and it would be like her parents." Ozzie stands and nods at Mel's bottle. "Want another?"

"No, thanks. I'm still working on this one."

"Okay if I have another?"

"Sure. You're not driving anywhere else tonight, right?"

"Nope. I don't have a car to drive." He enters the house through the sliding glass doors and emerges less than a minute later with a second bottle.

"How are you going to get to work in the morning?"

"Charlie can probably take me in." Ozzie settles back in his chair and takes a drink. "I don't have set hours."

"Why are you the one doing all the checks at the fire station?"

"Because I'm the one on the payroll."

"Ah. You're the Fire Chief." Mel smirks and almost empties her bottle.

"Yeah. I take care of everything at the station on a daily basis; the guys take turns doing it on the weekends. We all take turns standing duty at the station--one squad at a time. Mostly kids and young men."

"So, it's all men?"

Ozzie grins at her. "So far."

"I'm not volunteering."

"You sure?"

"Yeah. I'm sure. I have a bum leg that isn't real, remember? And I've got a job back in the city." Sort of. If she could get it back.

"They're letting you take this much time off?"

Mel shrugs. "I work at a vet center. Part-time as a scheduler." She snorts. "And part-time as a patient." She sniffs. "When I told them about my dad dying, they insisted I come home. Take all the time I need." The lie almost catches in her throat, but she chokes it down with a final swig of beer.

"Just because of your dad?" Ozzie taps his bottle against the chair arm. "Or is there something else?"

Shifting on the chair, Mel stares at the barely discernable tree line. "Yeah, there's something else. But I don't want to talk about it."

"Okay." Ozzie takes more of his beer. "Want me to keep talking?"

"Sure." She's relieved that he doesn't expect her to talk. She isn't sure she wants to know more about his marriage, though.

"When Joanie first asked for the separation—six years ago now—my mum stepped in to take the kids. I was not ready to take on that responsibility on my own. Joanie, well, she went back to school on a woman's scholarship and then got an MBA and is working for International Coal in West Virginia. The kids go visit four weeks every summer, and she comes here to see them at Christmas—they stay a week at her parents. She's trying to be the best mother she can be, but she's found her ambition."

"Oh. So now...?"

"We're getting the divorce, but it takes a while because we have children, even though my mother has effective custody. We're working on a plan that works for everybody. I'm trying to be a better dad, but I don't think I'm passing muster. Barry likes to spend time with me, but Lexie, she probably remembers more than Barry, but she doesn't want to spend a lot of time with me. Then, I worry, that Barry's biological father will show up and really put a kink in things."

"Damn." Mel sits forward. "Does Barry know?"

"Not yet. We're not sure what that knowledge would do to them. Neither of us wants to hurt them any more than we already have." Ozzie drains his second bottle.

Mel watches him for a moment, expecting him to go for a third beer, but he doesn't, simply settles the second bottle next to the first beside his chair.

"The divorce is almost settled."

"I'm sorry." Mel doesn't settle back. It's time to head back. "I should get back to the farm."

Ozzie stands, glaring at his empty bottles. "Yeah. Probably for the best."

"We can do this again. It was...nice." Mel stands, smiling but her stomach jumps and clenches. What does she expect?

"Good." Ozzie smiles back and runs a finger down her jaw line, the thumb brushing over her lower lip.

She wants him to kiss her. Taking in a quick breath, Mel licks over her lips, her tongue making contact with his skin.

Ozzie sucks in a breath and pushes his fingers into her hair, cupping the back of head. He makes no other move.

His skin is warm on hers. She shivers but doesn't move away.

He takes the hint.

Warm lips press against hers and Mel opens to them. Then, his tongue is there, too, and his other hand grips her hip. He crowds her space, but Mel doesn't panic.

Not like usual.

Not like the last time someone tried to kiss her. Though to be honest, she hadn't been expecting that kiss and had dropped her date to the deck in half a heartbeat.

Her hands move without her say-so, running over his stomach to meet behind him. She shifts closer, kissing him back.

When he pulls back to drag in air, "Mel?"

"Mmm? I thought you said you don't play?"

Ozzie stills. "Maybe this isn't playing."

Mel stiffens, her fingers curling into the fabric of his t-shirt. What is it if not playing? She stares up at him a long moment.

And then, his lips descend again, covering hers, his tongue dancing over her teeth, begging entrance.

She opens her mouth, accepting the invasion. Her fingers grip into his shirt, pulling at the fabric. The mewling sound in her throat surprises her.

His hands leave her hair, drifting, light as a breeze, down her neck and over her shoulders, then down her back to her bottom, caressing. They leave a heated path behind.

Grinding against him, Mel pulls him closer, pressing against him. It's like she can't get close enough, their clothes are in the way.

Ozzie moans, his hands gripping her bottom, pressing against her. He drags his lips away, gulping in air, then descends again, sucking and nibbling at the tender flesh of her mouth.

Mel nips back, sliding her tongue between his lips, her own breath coming in short pants when she can pull in air. A desperation builds inside; she tugs his shirt up and slips her hands beneath.

His flesh is warm, her fingers cool, and he shivers at the touch.

That only make Mel bolder; she snakes one hand up his side, bringing it forward to run her nails over his nipple. It tautens and he groans again.

"Mel." His voice whispers against her throat, the heat of the word making goosebumps erupt.

"Ozzie." She dips the fingers of the hand still behind him below the waistband of his jeans, her fingers pressing into the flesh.

"Oh, gods, Mel." Ozzie's hands grasp her between her bottom and her thighs, dragging her up his body. He sets her against the desk railing, wedging himself between her legs.

Gasping, Mel presses herself against him, against the growing bulge between his thighs.

His hands run down her thighs to her knees, cupping behind them—his fingers don't even pause at the prosthetic hinge—pulling her legs up and around him.

Mel pushes. No, not now. Too soon. Her leg...she couldn't let him see it, not while they are...

Headlights flare across the trees that line the road, tires crunch and the dull whine of an engine cuts off, then a door slams.

Mel gasps, her body going stiff. Panic flits through her muscles, automatically preparing to run, to hide, to attack. She breathes in slowly, willing her brain to take control, to decide that she's not on danger.

Ozzie freezes, his head tipped back. "Fuck. That's Charlie."

Keys jangle, the jarring in the otherwise quiet night, their labored breaths the only other sound.

The front door slams and a light flips on inside the house.

"I should leave." Mel shifts back, letting her legs drop. Her breath is shaky, and she hopes Ozzie thinks it's just from the kissing and not because she was ready to take his friend out of commission.

Ozzie wraps his arms around her, burying his face in her hot neck. "Yeah." He swallows and steps back, his hands dragging over her arms, clearing his throat.

Licking over her lips, tasting him and beer, Mel wishes she could stay, or invite Ozzie back to her place. But she can't. Her mother is there. Hell, it isn't even her place. She has problems. And Ozzie already has one mess. He doesn't need another one.

She slides off the deck rail, her knees a bit unsteady, so she grips the support behind her with her hands. "We could go for a run tomorrow." Where the hell has that offer come from? But she doesn't take it back.

Ozzie stares moment and smiles. "After work?"

"Sure." Mel steps away, stretching to cover the shakiness of her knees. "What time?"

"Like I said, my hours are pretty flexible." Ozzie leans a hip against the back of his Adirondack and crosses his arms.

Mel looks away. He looks too sexy, too easy. "Give me a call when you're done?"

"I will."

"Ozzie?" The deep voice from inside the house is vaguely familiar. Charlie appears in the doors, his face lighting up with a smile when he sees her. "Hey, Mel! How are you?"

Smiling, Mel shifts toward the steps down to the path that snakes around the garage. "I'm pretty good. You?"

Charlie shrugs. "Good as can be, I guess. Visiting?"

"Yeah." Mel pauses at the top of the steps. "I'll see you tomorrow, Ozzie. Nice seeing you again, Charlie."

Charlie's truck is parked next to the Miata, so Charlie had known someone was here. Is it usual for Ozzie to have a guest? Had Charlie seemed surprised to see someone?

Voices drifted in the dark. "So, where's your car?"

"Stalled out down the road. Mel gave me a lift."

"Huh."

Mel opens her car door and climbs in. She's not sure she's ready for confirmation of Ozzie's frequency of having guests, either way.

She has no trouble backing out and getting on the road, and in a few minutes, she's pulling into the drive of the farm. Sitting in the car, gazing up at the full moon hanging in the dark blue of the night, she wonders if it's time to come home for good.

§

"So where is home?" It was the Adjutant, a freckle-faced 2nd Lieutenant, whispering at her ear as they sat in the dirt next to the HUMVEE, eating not-quite-ready MREs.

"Virginia. Small town outside Richmond. Out by the river. A farm near Tappahannock. You?"

"Frederick, Maryland. That's where my mother is anyway, and where I graduated high school. I went to university in West Virginia, not far from home." The olive-skinned kid shoved a mouthful of mushy pasta in tomato sauce into his mouth.

"And your father?"

"Boston. But when I joined, he was living in Vermont with his boyfriend. When they broke up, he moved to Boston, into a condo near his work."

"Oh."

"Are your folks still together?"

"Yeah. I can't imagine them married to anyone else."

"That where you'll go when you go back?"

"What?" Mel choked on her peas and carrots in pseudo-beef gravy. She had never found a piece of real meat in any of the MREs she's eaten. "Um, no. I won't go there when I go back. I'll probably go wherever the Marines send me next."

"So, you're in for life?"

"That's my plan. Right now, anyway." Mel took a sip of her water and stirred her food. "I mean, I enlisted for the education benefits, stayed for the career." She doesn't mention that decision was pre-empted by the fight with her dad.

"Oh." The 2ndLt nodded. "I'm only in 'cause they paid for my degree. I figure I can make more money as an engineer in the private sector."

"Ah. Okay. I'm enlisted, remember?"

"Yeah, but they'll still pay for you to go to school. A couple of guys in my last battalion went to school while they were in."

"Oh." Mel finished her MRE and scrunched the disposable container into a tight ball. "I hadn't thought much about that. They trained me to be a mechanic, and I figured that's what I'd do. Until I get out, anyway."

Munching loudly, the kid spoke around the last of his lunch. "Well, don't forget about those benefits. You could at least finsh your lower-level credits."

"Yeah, yeah. You're a regular education brochure." Gunney stood over them, machine gun in hand.

"What's wrong with getting an education?" The 2nd Lieutenant wasn't cowed by the older man.

"Don't need one in the Marines."

"Yeah, well, a lot of Marines don't get to stay in. And getting an education is a decent fall-back plan." The Adjutant stood and picked up his own weapon. He nodded at Mel and stalked away, tossing his lunch debris in a trash bag hanging from the side of a transport.

Gunney snorted. "Love these kids. They think they know so much." He spit into the dirt. "Give him a couple years' experience and we'll see what he has to say about that shit."

Mel didn't say anything. She understood where the 2ndLt was coming from. Education was why she'd enlisted—mostly that and to see some of the world, escape the small town she'd been born in, discover herself. There hadn't been a lot of money for school, and student loan debt hadn't been something she wanted. Maybe, if her dad hadn't gone off like a mad gorilla at her, she might have stuck to that plan. She was a competent mechanic, but was it enough?

# 12

### REPAIRS

"Yeah, Sheldon drove it in last night." Gary's voice crackles over the old phone line. "I've got the hood up now. Looks like it's the carburetor."

"That's what I thought." Mel wonders if Delta had passed on her message or if Gary had been left to do all the checking from scratch.

"Saw your note. All I did was confirm it. Want me to order one in?"

"Can you check over the rest of it? See if there's anything else that needs to be fixed?"

"Sure. You planning on fixing everything?"

"Wondering if it's worth it or if I should see about getting Ma a new truck. I'll pay for the labor of checking it over if we decide to get a new one."

"Sure. You want me to check over the body and stuff, too?"

"I think that's a good idea."

"Your Dad kept that truck in working condition. I don't expect to find anything much wrong with it."

"When did he bring it in last? Has Ma had it in for you to look at since he passed?"

A moment of silence along the line makes Mel think the connection has dropped. But then, "No, she hasn't. I'll take a long look over it and let you know."

"Thanks, Gary." Mel hangs up and sighs, resting her forehead against the cool wall. The faded cherries and bananas and what could be grapes on the wallpaper are all in weird, bleary focus with her eyes so close. She wonders what else should be looked at or checked.

"Something wrong, dear?" Ma asks from the arch that leads to the den. The muted sounds of a game show reverberate in the background.

"No, not really. Just asking Gary to make some extra checks on the truck while it's in the shop." Mel straightens and smiles at her mother.

Blinking, Ma stares a moment before turning to head back to the den. "Come sit with me for a bit."

Mel grabs a mug and fills it with tea, then obeys and finds her way to the second recliner. She doesn't recognize the game show on the TV.

Ma sets the footrest in the up position on her recliner and mutes the TV. "Can we talk for a minute?"

"Sure."

Turning to face her mother, Mel sets her mug on the table. This must be serious. Her mother hadn't used that tone with her since the birds and the bees discussion when Mel was thirteen.

"I think I should move into town.appahannock. There's a small apartment building with cute little one-bedroom apartments and an elevator if you need it. It's near the river."

This isn't what she's expecting. "So, you want to sell the farm?" Dad would scream in his grave.

"No, but I can't keep up with it anymore." Ma watches the host on the TV wave his hand while the contestant jumps and screams in silence. They must have won whatever game they were playing.

"What does Brad think?"

"I haven't talked to him about it. But I can't imagine he'd be upset. He has his house—with that damn in-law suite—and never comes to see me out here. Says it's too far away for a quick visit. But I don't want to live with him and Chrissie."

Mel considers her mother's profile. "You want me to take the farm?"

Ma's head jerks in Mel's direction. "Do you want the farm?"

Shrugging, Mel sips her tea. "I don't know. What will happen to your animals?"

The deep, exaggerated sigh brings Mel's head around. Ma's eyes are closed and her lips are pressed tight together. "I don't know."

"Let's think about that, then, okay?" Mel isn't sure how she feels about the possibility of her mother selling the farm. It has been 'home' for a long time, even though she hasn't been here for more than fifteen years. No matter what she'd told that 2nd Lieutenant a lifetime ago: this is *home*.

"I'm sure I can find someone to take the sheep and the cows." Ma nods and sips from her own mug. "Mr. Wallace has sheep and won't mind a few more. He keeps a decent-sized flock and sells wool to a high-end craft shop outside Richmond and one in Virginia Beach. He might take the cows, too."

"And the monster from hell?"

"Herbert, the llama? He's not a monster." Ma clucks her tongue and waves a hand. "You need to gain his trust, Mel. He's a very cautious creature."

"Cautious my ass. He damn near bit me yesterday." Mel sinks back in her Dad's recliner.

"Watch your language, young lady."

Mel snorts. "Ma, I've been talking like this since I got back, with no complaints from you. And I'm not a young lady anymore."

"Well, you're not an old lady."

But some days, she feels like it. Mel uncurls her right leg, stretching it out next to the left. Her right foot is bare, the resin one covered in the rubberized sock. She sighs.

"What?"

"Brad offered to have us over for dinner at his house. We should probably call and take him up on it. We can discuss the farm and your apartment then."

"Discuss?" Ma raises a brow.

"Relay your decision to him, then."

"That's better."

Yes, some days, Mel feels absolutely ancient.

§

Mel felt old, watching the young kids, still pimpled virgins, staring wide-eyed and pissed-pants out at the hardscape of war. These kids were in charge, having a commission and a degree.

They were doomed.

"Shit, look at the scrawny punks." Gunney spat on the ground. "I swear they're getting younger every group they fly in."

Shrugging, Mel stuck her head back in the engine compartment of the stalled truck. It was a convoy of three trucks and two HUMVEEs, and the middle truck didn't look like it was making it back to base. "One of the belts snapped. Lucky it didn't take out the radiator when it went."

"Can you fix it?"

"Got a spare belt on you?"

Gunney just stared.

"Didn't think so." Mel turned to one of the newbies. "You got a spare belt in your pack?"

"Huh? Yeah, I think so."

"Can you get to it?" Mel nodded at the back of the truck where the packs were tucked beneath the benches and lined down the middle.

"Sure." The kid jumped into the back and rummaged throughout one of the large sacks, pulling out a long green webbed belt and shiny buckle. "Here."

"Thanks." Mel tugged it, testing its strength. "Remind me that we owe you a new belt. You won't want this one back."

"Okay." The kid followed, watching her string the webbed length of fabric around the two bare pulleys and use duct tape to cinch them together.

"Take your buckle. We probably won't have one that shiny for you on base." Mel tested the tautness of the makeshift part before straightening and slamming the hood shut. "Let's see if she'll run long enough to make it to base."

"Load up!" Gunney hollered and jumped to the back of the truck.

Everyone hustled and within a minute the trucks were started and rumbling along the dirt road, the one in the middle stuttering but moving. By the time they made it through the gates, the odor of burning cotton filled the cab, but Mel just kept her head hanging out the window.

# 13

## RUN, RUN, RUN

The ringing phone is a welcome distraction. They've run out of animals to talk about and the game show makes no sense to Mel at all. "I'll get it." She jumps from the recliner, setting her mug on the side table. "Maybe it's Gary."

It isn't Gary; it's Ozzie.

"You ready to go for a run?"

Mel glances at the wall clock hanging above the sink: it's three o'clock. "Sure."

"I'll be there in half an hour. We running out the old road?"

"We can, I guess." Traffic shouldn't be a worry out that way. Mel frowns. "What car are you driving?"

"I'm borrowing my mother's Cadillac. Sheldon was out to grab the junker and take it into Gary early this morning. I saw the truck when I was over about the car."

"Yeah. I guess Sheldon dropped it off last night some-time."

"How much is it going to be for a new carburetor?"

"Still waiting on that. I asked Gary to look over the rest of it first."

"Oh." A heavy metal door slams and an engine purrs to life. "Well, I should be there in thirty minutes. I have my running gear with me, but I'll have to change."

"Okay, I'll be ready." Mel hangs up and turns to find her mother watching her again.

"Ready for what?"

"Ozzie's coming by. We're going for a run."

"A run?" Her mother glances down at her bum leg. "Mel... can you?"

"Yeah. Well, not for long. Probably wind up walking, but it's exercise. Down the old road. Maybe through the field if the trail is still there." When she'd been a kid, Mel and Brad, and a couple other kids had used to ride down a dirt bike trail through the woods and fields, it had been a shortcut between back yards and the back woods.

"His car get fixed before the truck?" Ma's deepening frown betrays the unspoken privilege the Manley's took for granted.

"No. He's borrowing his mother's car."

"Ah. Maisie has an apartment in town. Probably doesn't need her car on a daily basis. We'd be neighbors if I moved in town." The frown is gone and Ma is back to watching the TV.

Mel nods but says nothing, shuffling past to head for the stairs.

"How long will you be gone?"

"Depends on how far we go." Upstairs, Mel grabs her duffle to dig through the still unpacked sweat pants, running shorts, and t-shirts—all in standard Marine Corps green. It's warm out, and she'll only get warmer running, so she throws on a T-shirt and shorts, then pulls on socks and a worn sneaker, leaving the running prosthetic, with its rubber and resin "foot", bare.

Sitting on the bed, she stares down at her thighs. With her feet tucked against the bed, it only looks like she's got a knee brace on her leg. No reason to believe half her left leg is gone.

She sticks her legs out, the muscles in her thighs tightening and standing out beneath her skin. The muscles in the right don't match the left; they aren't less defined, just shaped differently. The weight of the prosthetic has changed the rest of the left leg.

The sweatpants are draped over the chair, beckoning. If she wears the pants, she—and Ozzie—wouldn't have to look at the contraption that is now hers. She could pretend to be whole, complete, not broken.

It's tempting. There's an allure to the illusion.

But this is *Ozzie*. Something inside taunts her that Ozzie needs to see the real her, more real than just the leg. He's interested—hell, so is she—in some kind of relationship, even just a physical one. Shouldn't he know what he's getting into?

Standing, she takes a deep breath and moves to the hall and down the stairs, letting her fingers brush the soft knit of the pants. She doesn't grab them, though her fingers flex when she passes through the door.

Downstairs, Ma stands at the sink, looking out the window at the overgrown garden. "It's too much."

Mel stays quiet, right foot still on the last step, one hand braced against the wall.

"I can't keep up with everything." It sounds like Ma is crying.

"We can go into town tomorrow and you can show me one of these apartments." Mel doesn't know what to do. Should she offer a hug?

Ma nods but doesn't turn around.

The sound of car wheels on gravel reaches them.

"That will be Ozzie. He needs to change into his running gear." Mel wants her mother to turn around, to see the leg, all of it, what's left of it. But she stays looking out the window, and Mel is scared to make her turn around. Just in case.

An engine cuts off and seconds later, a car door slams. Ozzie whistles on his way to the door. When he knocks, Mel pauses, waiting for her mother to tell her it's okay to let him in.

Ma sighs. "I'm good, Mel. He doesn't need to stand out there waiting." She swipes over her face and heads for the stairs, not really seeing Mel—or her leg. "I think I'm going to lay down for a bit."

"Okay." Mel watches her mother ascend to the second floor before opening the door to a frowning Ozzie.

"What's up?" He glances down but his eyes come right back up again.

Shrugging, Mel steps aside. "Ma is... I don't know. I'll tell you on our run." She waves at the downstairs half bath. "Go ahead and change. You need water?"

"You mean a bottle for our run? Sure." Ozzie answers through the door and Mel gets two empty metal water canisters to fill from the tap. The house uses well water, and as far as Mel is concerned, it's better than anything ever purchased in plastic.

The small basement studio in a Virginia Beach townhouse felt huge—cavernous compared to a shared Quonset quad. It had a combined living room and kitchenette—the bed tucked in a corner behind a heavy curtain—and a bathroom—all to herself. It was quiet, no hum of generator or whispered conversation, no thump of music escaping the listeners' earbuds.

No rocket fire or rat-a-tat of machine gun. No faint odor of stale piss or rotting excrement. No engine thrum of HUMVEE or helicopter.

She had a full-size bed draped in a fluffy blue comforter. Matching sham covers decorated the pillows. A shaggy cream throw was draped over the end.

"I hope you like it." Glenne stood, staring at Mel. "I remembered you liked blue in high school."

"Yeah. The color is fine." Mel wandered around the room, running fingers over the top of the dresser set against the wall at the foot, testing the texture of the darker blue curtain-wall.

There was a couch and flatscreen in the living room, a side chair and rug. Pictures on the wall. More pillows. Three stools at the breakfast bar in the kitchenette.

It set a modern tone. Cool colors in blue, gray, and black. She'd have loved it in high school.

Glenne watched her. "You sure?"

Mel sighed. "It's great Glenne. I'm just..." How could she explain? She'd been forward deployed since basic training and A school. She hadn't had a place of her own since she'd left home.

"It can all go back and you can get something else. You didn't give me much to go on."

Mel turned to face her friend. Glenne still looked like Glenne—only older: chic and polished and successful. "This is more than I expected. I figured you'd find me somewhere to stay and I'd have to go buy my own stuff."

"I wanted you to have a bed when you got here." Glenne's voice sounded choked and Mel reached out and grabbed her hand.

"Thank you. It really is great, Glenne." And if Mel faced the truth, if Glenne hadn't gotten her a bed, she'd be sleeping on the floor for at least a month, if not longer.

"Okay."

They were silent a moment.

"I got you a bit of food. Just the basics. Bread, eggs, milk. Deli turkey and cheese so you can have a sandwich. Coffee and cream and sugar."

Mel laughed. "You always were an organizer."

"Still am. It's what I'm paid to do." Glenne grinned and opened the compact fridge with a flourish. "Voila."

Hugging her friend, Mel closed her eyes and for a moment, she was a teen again and she and Glenne were playing house while her parents were off for the weekend. Yawning, she rubbed her face over her friend's shoulder. "I'm sorry. Long drive."

"I'm sure." Glenne hugged her back, squeezing tight. " I95 is a right mess in the summer. Makes a three-hour drive three times as long."

"Thanks for everything." She'd rented only a room on base the six months she'd lasted in Quantico. An old woman ran a boarding house by the river, all the rooms furnished, utilities included. Mel hadn't needed anything else.

"Thanks for deciding to relocate here."

Mel pulled back and shrugged. "It's a military town. I should be able to find a job. There's a vet center in Hampton. Not too hard for me to get to rehab." The desk job at Quantico had meant therapy was a day trip to Fort Belvoir.

"How's your leg?" Glenne looked down at the jean-covered limb, like she might be able to see through the heavy fabric.

Talking about it meant she thought about it, so now it throbbed, the stub pulsing, the faint feeling of something below ghosting at her. "Starting to feel it." She refused to rub it, though.

"I'll let you settle and get to bed then. See you tomorrow? I'll take you out for breakfast and grocery shopping."

Laughing, the sound weak and tired, Mel nodded. "I'm almost asleep now."

Glenne gave her one last hug and left out the door, waving before closing it behind her. "Don't forget to lock up."

"I won't." Mel walked to the door and slid the chain across and flipped the little dial in the knob.

Alone, she listened to the quiet. All she could hear was faint music from the upstairs neighbor's TV.

Yawning again, she grabbed her purse—something else awkward to carry—digging through to find the little bottle of pills prescribed by the German doctor and still filled by the military healthcare system. They helped her sleep.

She stared at the pills. The label said to take one an hour before bed. What would happen if she took two? Three?

Mel shook the pills into her palm, rolling them around, feeling their slight weight, then put all but one back in the container. She wasn't that far gone yet.

She opened a cupboard door to find plates and bowls, mugs and glasses inside. Checking a drawer, she found silverware. There were probably pots and pans somewhere, too.

Glenne had taken care of everything for her.

Taking a glass down, she flipped the cold tap and watched the water rush from the tap. It was cool and she filled the glass.

Popping the pill in her mouth, she took a gulp of water and swallowed.

"Gagh." Chlorine. She'd almost prefer the warm piss water of the base in Afghanistan.

# 14

## LET'S TALK AWHILE

The run feels good, the heat in her leg muscles, the air hard in her lungs. She'd forgotten how free she felt running. How powerful, accomplished—in control.

The edge of the Velcro bites into the flesh of her thigh and she slows to a walk to adjust it.

Ozzie stops with her. He's been loping beside her, matching his naturally longer gait to her shorter stride. Breathing easy, sweat trickles down his temples and neck, wetting the collar of his t-shirt.

"Sorry." Starting again, Mel speeds up, getting a little ahead of him. He stays behind, letting her lead. Their feet hit the pavement in sync, right-left right-left, a steady thuck-thuck-thuck to keep them going. Though she's more thuck-tink-thuck-tink.

Rounding a wide turn, a deer stands in the middle of the road, an older yearling with her.

Stopping, Mel raises her hands above her head and pumps her knees up and down, the Velcro pinching hard at the violent twisting. Ozzie stops, too, making the same moves to keep the air coming into his lungs.

The doe stares a moment, frozen in the road. The yearling, not understanding the possible danger, keeps crossing, wading into the swaying grass. Its mother joins him, her eyes never leaving the pair of panting humans.

"Probably lucky it wasn't a bear." Ozzie is breathless.

"Probably."

"Want to run again, or tell me what's up with your mom?"

"Is that an excuse to take a break?" Mel takes a deep breath, stretching her arms up and back to make her lungs bigger.

"Could be."

Mel stares at him a moment. "I'll take it." She adjusts the cup and Velcro again, checking the stump for extra redness and chafing.

"Everything okay?" Ozzie watches, hands on his hips, chests expanding and contracting with each deep pant.

Looking up, she eyes his face. There is no revulsion, only curiosity and slight concern.

"I think so." She tests the fit by bending her knee a little and starts walking. "Ma wants to move in town. She says the farm is getting too much for her."

Ozzie strolls beside he, his longer gait keeping their footfalls out of sync. He looks out into a field where the two deer are almost invisible. "My aunt—Dad's sister—bought one of those retirement apartments. It's a one-bedroom, all on one level. The mayor built a couple of three-story complexes where the old fishing warehouse used to be."

"Bought?"

"Yeah. More like took a share of the building, I guess. I admit, I'm not sure exactly how that all works. When she dies, someone else can buy in and her estate will receive the money, minus a fee for the mayor, of course."

Mel nods, but doesn't understand.

"Doctor Watkins visits everyone once a week, and a nurse is on call if they need anything. Not a bad deal, I guess."

"So, it's like assisted living?" Mel starts walking back toward the farm.

Ozzie follows, doing torso twists and high knees. "I guess. Except they buy in."

"Well, that doesn't sound so bad."

"What about the farm?"

Mel rolls her eyes and shrugs. "Don't know. If she has to buy into the apartment, I guess she'll have to sell it."

"How do you feel about that?" Ozzie stops.

Sighing, Mel shakes her head. "Until she said it, I would have said I'd be fine with it. But, once she mentioned it...it felt wrong. Like I wouldn't have a place to go. Which is stupid; I have my apartment." Well, she didn't, not anymore, but she could find another one.

"Yeah. I guess I know how you feel. That's why I always figured I'd buy Mum's house when she was done with it. But, with the kids, and everything..." His voice trails off and he clears his throat. "But Aunt Maisie is happy enough with the place. And the in-house doctor checks her meds and her blood pressure every week. It's less of a worry for everyone."

So, maybe Ma moving would be a good thing. Not only would someone be monitoring her health, but she'd be closer to folks her own age, be able to visit and do things with her friends. Have someone to watch the game shows with. And she wouldn't need the truck or the old car; could probably buy a compact with better gas mileage.

"I brought up the animals. I don't think she has a plan for them yet." Mel opens her water bottle and takes a drink. The water is warm now, but it still tastes cleansing in her mouth.

"Minor issue." Ozzie waves his water bottle at her. "I'm sure you can find someone to take them in."

"Even Herbert-the-llama? From the way Ma tells it, she was the only one willing to take him in before."

Squinting, Ozzie wrinkles his nose. "He may be a problem. The vet thought he was going to have to put him down before your mother made her offer."

The rumble of an engine moves them into the grass and dirt on the side of the road. Ozzie waves at the driver of a new Ford 150, who honks in reply.

Mel raises a brow.

"Will Weston. He bought a couple of acres from old Mr. Mackinaw and built a new house on it."

"What does he do?"

"He runs the new bank in Tappahannock. Newish brick building right on Main. Married the mayor's daughter. The younger one. I can't remember her name. I think she was two years behind us in school."

Nodding, Mel focuses on the possibilities ahead. If her mother moves out of the farm, would she go back to an apartment? She'd have to; she had nowhere else to go when she went back.

If she went back.

But Ma would be closer to Brad and Chrissie. Brad could check on her, visit more often. She'd be close to friends, old and new.

There wouldn't be as much for Mel to worry about.

But what if those worries are what kept her in the here and now? What gives her purpose? What would she do then?

She feels lost, like when she'd first left the Marines, been told she was being sep'ed, that she's lost her leg and had to figure out her life from then on out.

The VA hadn't helped much, though volunteering had made her feel a little less lost. It hadn't been enough. And some of the stories, the reasons for others' lost limbs had made her feel guilty that she'd only been bit by a viper and a kid had tied her leg off too tight.

She thought of the damn llama. Is that how it felt? Lost? How would it feel if it had to move again? What if no one took him in?

Does she want it? She doesn't think so, but at the same time, she doesn't want the damn thing put down.

"Maybe I'll stay for a bit. Take care of it."

"It?" Ozzie freezes with his water bottle half-way to his mouth.

"The llama, Herbert. Make sure someone takes him in." Mel shrugs and shifts. The Velcro bites sharp into her skin but she ignores it. "It will give me a purpose."

"A purpose?" He lowers the bottle, licking his lips.

Mel takes his arm, facing him full on, keeping his gaze on her.

His gaze crashes into hers.

"I have a diagnosis of PTSD, Ozzie. I'm broken and I need a band-aid. A big one." Mel swallows and blinks away the wet from her eyes. "I volunteered at the VA until I heard that Dad was gone. Then, all I could think about was coming home. I told everyone, and me, that this wasn't home anymore. But it is. And I'm scared to lose it. That if I do, I'll lose what's left of me, too."

She can't deny the tears anymore and lets them fall. She tries to swallow and chokes.

Ozzie takes her hand, losing the bottle but ignoring where it lands and spills, and pulls her close, wraps his warm arms around her and rocks her side to side.

Mel expects to resist the embrace, for her hackles to rise and the desire to run to overwhelm her muscles. When it doesn't, she relaxes and burrows closer, winding her own arms around him and clinging in a way she hasn't clung to anyone in almost fifteen years.

His lips brush her temple. "It's okay. I've got you, Mel."

Sobbing, she squeezes tighter. "What do I do?"

"You want to take care of the llama, take care of the llama. But think about this, maybe that won't be enough. It won't take long to take care of it. An hour a day at most."

Mel jerks back. "You don't want me to take care of Herbert?"

"Yes, I want you to take care of Herbert. But you'll get bored pretty quick with only him. Bored even with the other animals. I think that's part of your mother's problem. It isn't enough for all day." Ozzie rubs his hands over her back, not letting her get any farther away. "And what about the PTSD? If you stay here, what will you do about that?"

Guilt crashes over her. She'd mentioned the PTSD. She's a Marine. It has to be from the fighting, that's what the VA thinks. And the war is some of it...probably. That's where her nightmares come from, most of them.

But the real problem for her isn't the war. Oh, it's part of it, but the part that is killing her now is the part she can't talk about.

"What else can I do?"

"What about working at the garage?"

Mel looks up and she's close—really close—to Ozzie. She can see the pulse beating in his neck, the glisten of sweat on his skin; smell an odor that is not entirely unpleasant, musky and sweaty and salty. "You mean, be a mechanic?"

"So far, Gary works alone. He's hired a couple of kids, mostly in summers, but they don't stick around. Head off to school for something better. And Delta isn't going to do it."

Closing her eyes, Mel thinks she can block him out, but she can't. His hands are warm and firm, his breath whispers along her cheek. "Ozzie."

"Stay here, Mel. Not just until Herbert has a home. He has a home. Stay so he can stay."

*Stay.*

Could she? Should she? "How? I think Ma needs to sell the farm to get an apartment."

"Talk to her. She just needs a reason to stay at the farm."

"I'm not sure I'm a good reason. She worries about me when I have a nightmare. She wants me to talk to her about it."

"Then talk to her."

"I can't."

"Why not?"

Mel opens her eyes to find Ozzie's face right there, close enough she's breathing in his exhales. "I'm scared."

"Why?" Ozzie leans closer, his lips brushing her cheek. "She's your mother."

"I killed people, well, shot at them, made them bleed if I hit them." *They'd probably died.* "How can I tell my mother about that?" Mel's voice shakes and she can't steady it. More lies. Oh, it is truth that she's done those things, but she could probably talk to her mother about that. She'd been a Marine, doing her job. There should be no shame in that.

"I guess you can't. But you can tell me. In fact, you just did." Ozzie pulls her close again and she melds against him, letting him hold her up. "I've seen things, too."

"Have you killed someone?"

"No. But I've seen folks die. When I could have saved them if I'd been faster or stronger." Ozzie's voice is gruff and it rumbles into her neck.

That might be worse. Mel brings her head up, focusing on Ozzie's face through watery eyes. "Does talking help you?"

"Don't know. Haven't tried it."

"Tell you what, then, we'll both talk, okay? And go from there?"

"Sure." Ozzie presses his lips into her neck, squeezing her tight before letting go. He takes her hand, winding her fingers through his, and tugging her along.

They walk the rest of the way back to the farm, quiet but calm. Mel wonders if this is what being content feels like. If this might work; if working with Gary and talking care of that damn llama might be what she needs.

She could tell her mother, and see what happens. If Ma still wants to sell the farm and move into town, maybe she could borrow the money to buy it. She has some money put away; she should be able to use a VA loan since she had those benefits.

It's dusk when they turn down the drive. Mel's legs are jelly; it's been a while since she'd run and then walked. The stump throbs; she'll need to gauze it up before bed. But the inner peace, or at least the current cease fire, is worth the pain.

The kitchen light is on, spilling through the window onto the green of the lawn. Ma must be up from her nap, probably making dinner.

"Ma?" Once inside, Mel drops Ozzie's hand. He doesn't protest, just follows her inside.

"In the kitchen."

Mel leads the way to the kitchen, sniffing the air that is awash in the aroma of pot roast and biscuits. "Dinner?"

"I made enough for three. I hope Ozzie plans to stay." Ma leans back, smiling at their guest.

"Yes, ma'am. I admit, I was hoping you'd ask." Ozzie grins.

"Well, both of you clean up. Ozzie, you have something to change into? You can use the downstairs shower off the mud room if you like." Ma pulls a Dutch oven from the oven, placing it on a trivet on the counter. "It's almost ready. The biscuits are already out. All I have to do it set the table."

Ozzie picks up his gym bag and backs up into the mud room. "I'll be done in two shakes."

Ma turns from the stove, her smile faltering when she sees Mel. Her gaze drops to the prosthetic and she swallows.

Standing still, Mel waits. She can't help the tightening of her muscles, the stiffening of her spine.

"You should wear shorts more often." Ma takes a breath and grins at her. "Your legs are awful pale. They need some sun."

Ma turns back to the cupboards and pulls plates and glasses down, humming under her breath.

Blinking, Mel turns and heads upstairs. For the moment, she's normal and whole. She could talk to her mother; not about everything, but about some of it, about Gunney and the drinking and the whatever it was that they did in the end.

And then, maybe she could tell Ozzie.

§

"How much have you had to drink?" Gunney stands at the end of her cot, hands on hips, cover in hand.

"Not enough." Mel spoke from beneath her pillow. "Go away. I'm on liberty hours."

"You're drunk."

"Nope. Not even close." She threw the pillow aside, the glare from the lamps making her squint her eyes. "Trust me, I did not drink enough to get drunk."

"You reek of alcohol."

"I spilled some on me."

"Then get up and take a shower."

"No. I told you, I'm on liberty hours. I want to sleep."

"I said get up." Gunney kicked the end of the cot, the top bunk rattling.

Mel didn't move from the rack. "You want me up? Find someone in charge to tell me to get up. I told you, I'm on liberty."

"You-"

"Get out, Gunney. Don't make me report you." Mel didn't look at him, focusing on the metal slats making creases in the mattress above.

"Report me?" Gunney slaps his cap against the foot of her cot.

"Harassment. I'm on liberty. I can stay in my cot if I want."

"I want you to-"

"Gunney!" The 2nd Lieutenant's call halted the tirade. "Get out here!"

Mel was relieved. She was tired of the fight, tired of Gunney not leaving her alone. Tired of being in Afghanistan. Of the war, of carrying a gun everywhere.

And she wanted to shave her legs and wear a mini skirt and heels. Put some makeup on after taking a long soak in a bubble bath instead of a two-minute shower with three other women.

She sat up, staring at the hole in her right sock that let her big toe peek out. Wiggling all ten, she tucked the digit back into the green fabric. She has another bottle of pilfered wine in her locker. She could finish it off in the head, hiding the empty in the towel cart. Someone would find it, but they'd never figure out who put it there.

No one had said anything about the empties yet.

# 15

## WORSE THAN SHE THOUGHT

The next morning at the shop, Gary gives her the low-down on the truck. Yes, it needs a new carburetor. But it also needs new brakes and a master cylinder.

Mel considers the vehicle. Her dad had bought it new, off the lot, picking a color that her mother would like. It is a work horse, hauling feed and dirt and kids all over the farm. It's covered in dents and holes and rust.

"How much to fix it?"

"Probably close to three thou. That's just parts, not including labor." Gary runs a finger down the sheet. "Labor is thirty bucks an hour. Once I add that in, the truck's probably not worth that much money."

"Well, go ahead and order the parts."

"Order the parts?"

"Yeah. I can pay you for the diagnostic, and have it towed out to the farm. I can do the work."

"Even the master cylinder? You need big tools for that." Gary leans on the counter, adjusting the cap back on his balding head.

Mel rubs her fingers over her eyes. He's right. She needs a real garage to replace that part of the engine.

"I can let you use one of the bays here in the evenings, if you want. Unless I get another job in, which isn't likely."

"One of the bays?"

"Yeah." Gary takes his cap off and rubs his head. "I do it for the high school shop kids sometimes, when they don't finsh their project car before summer. We pull it in when I close down, and pull it back out in the morning."

"Okay. I'll use a bay. Thanks."

"You don't have to pay for another tow, either." Gary slaps the ball cap back on his head and makes a note on the top of the sheet. "I'll order these tomorrow. Not sure when they'll come in."

"Thanks."

"No problem."

"Hey, Gary?" Mel stops at the door, one hand on the plate metal next to the full-length glass panel.

"Yeah." Gary is frowning over papers behind the counter.

"You hiring?"

Gary's head snaps up. "You looking?"

"I think so." Mel steps back and returns to the counter. "I mean, if I stick around, I'll need a job."

"You need a job, I'm hiring." Gary sets the papers down.

"I've only got one and a half legs."

Gary raises a brow.

"I mean. I'm disabled. I have a prosthetic on my left leg. From the knee down."

"So?" Gary leans on the counter. "Haven't seen it stopping you so far."

Mel smirks. "Just want transparency, that's all. I swear like a sailor, too."

"A sailor, huh?"

She shrugs. "Well, like a Marine anyway. That might be worse."

He chuckles. "Like I said, if you're looking, I'm hiring."

"When you want me to start?"

Gary glances at the paper then leans to look around her at the first bay; the second is empty. "How about once you get the truck fixed? Give you a chance to think it over."

"I think I've thought it over."

"What about pay?"

Mel laughs. She hasn't considered that aspect of it. "How about I come in tomorrow morning and we talk about all that?"

"Sure. Six am?"

"How about 7?" She has to take care of the animals first. "Maybe half past?"

"That'll work. Delta will have the coffee made by then."

§

They'd asked her to make the coffee. Mel had never made it before, always finding the dark brew her mother made every morning for her father far too strong to be interested in it. She'd dumped half the can of coffee into the filter, the result more mud than liquid.

They'd banned her from ever touching the coffee pot again.

Which suited her just fine. She wasn't there to make coffee; she was a mechanic, her job was to fix engines.

She started out holding tools, the male mechanics asking for a wrench when it was obvious they needed a screwdriver. Mel would sigh, hand them the correct tool, and drum her fingers on the metal of the fender, waiting for the next test.

It took six months for them to decide she might know what she was doing and let her take a maintenance job on a Jeep. An oil change, not hard at all, except someone had decided to hide the proper grade of oil, so she'd had to hunt for it.

When she found it—on the highest shelf and behind a box of air filters—she'd worked into the evening to get it done by morning, not saying anything about finding the oil.

From the morning smirks, Mel could tell they thought she'd messed it up. On the one hand, they deserved their comeuppance, but on the other—it might only make it worse for her.

The Lieutenant Colonel who arrived to pick it up took it for a quick spin around the lot before signing the paperwork to take it back into his custody, and praising them for a well-done job—he swore it even drove better.

Mel laughed, accepting the paperwork back. "The tires were a bit out of round, so I did an alignment on the tires. No big deal; the tires will last longer."

The Lieutenant Colonel clapped her on the shoulder, asked for her name, and left.

The other mechanics sat on their stools, mouths agape, not saying a word.

Performing an exaggerated eye-batting, Mel addressed her fellow Marines. "Oh—and you might want to pull the rest of that oil down off that top shelf. I got enough down to do the oil change, but couldn't manage the rest of the crate, being a girl and all." And she swaggered off to perform the next maintenance routine on another Jeep in the bay.

That had been enough. She'd been put in regular rotation, performing maintenance and repairs like the rest of the mechanics, earning a bit of extra respect when her smaller frame let her fit into tighter spaces in the engine compartment and she figured out that the Colonel's HUMVEE rattled because of a loose nut on an engine mount.

And when she started drinking the coffee—with plenty of cream and sugar—the Master Sergeant gave her a mug that said "FE-male" on it.

# 16

## LLAMA DRAMA

Herbert hates her. The llama won't let her near him, won't eat the food she puts in his feed trough, won't come in from the field when she opens the door to the barn.

Mel glares at the animal, wondering at its stubborn stupidity. Would it really starve so it didn't have to come near her?

Well, she can be stubborn, too.

She leaves it outside, the barn door open and welcoming. She can check on it later. If he isn't in then, she'll lasso his ass and drag him in.

"Not going so well?" Ma stands at the sink, rinsing the last of the dishes from dinner.

"No. I can't imagine what that stupid creature is thinking." Mel slumps into a chair, leaning over the table, resting her forehead against its cool surface.

"It took him a while to warm up to me, too." A timer beeps and Ma opens the oven, releasing the aroma of freshly baked molasses cookies.

"I think I've gained ten pounds since I got here." Mel grins at her mother, anticipating the warm sweetness of the treats. "Not that I'm complaining, mind you. I just need to work out more." *Maybe let her pants out.*

"Ozzie would appreciate if you included him on that. I think he likes running."

"Yeah, he likes running." Laughing, Mel stands and grabs two mugs from the cupboard. "Tea or milk?"

"I'll take tea." Ma places a plate piled high with cookies on the table.

Mel puts a tea bag in one mug and tops it with hot water, then grabs the jug of milk from the fridge and pours some into the other. "Did you call about the apartment today?"

"Yes. I have an appointment at two tomorrow." Ma takes the mug of tea and a cookie and sits.

"You call Brad?"

"I called the house and left a message with Chrissie. He hasn't called back yet."

"Okay." Mel sips her milk. "I start work at the garage in the morning."

Ma almost drops her teacup, spilling her tea. She stares then sets the cup on the table, grabbing a paper towel to sop up the mess. "Work?"

"Yeah. I figure I'm gonna need a paycheck." Mel sets her mug on the table and sits, rimming the top with her finger. "I'm gonna need that to buy the farm."

Ma sits across from her, leaning forward. "You don't have to buy the farm. If you want it, it's yours."

"How will you pay for the apartment?"

Smiling, Ma reaches out a hand, gripping over Mel's. "Your father left a sizable insurance settlement. He did like his life insurance. I didn't have to spend much of it. The farm was already paid for, so was the truck and he'd paid cash for the car."

"What about Brad?"

"What about him?" Ma pulls her hand back to pick up a cookie.

"Will he be upset that I get it?"

"I don't think so. But we can ask." Ma bites into her cookie, eyes crinkling with her smile.

Mel's insides warm. It has been so long since she'd seen Ma's whole face smile like that. She doesn't want to ruin that, but she must. Before she loses her nerve.

She licks her lips and picks up her own cookie, breaking it in two but not eating any. "There was a guy in Afghanistan."

"A guy?" Ma sips her tea. She has no idea what's coming. "The one you mentioned before?"

"Yeah, that one. But, it was bad. The relationship wasn't healthy." Mel swallows and breaks the cookie into quarters, crumbs littering the tablecloth beneath.

"Mel?"

"I thought he was the one. That the trouble was worth it for him." She loses her voice and clears her throat, setting the destroyed cookie on the table. Blinking, she swipes at her eyes. "He was using me. There were others. For him, anyway. I don't think they mattered, either. And in the end, when I'd wised up and said no, he didn't accept it."

Ma stills, her fingers gripping tight to her cup, her knuckles white. She's staring, her eyes searching, finding. "Didn't accept it? Mel, did he...?"

Mel nods; she can't speak the words, not yet. She's not certain her mother is asking the right question.

"Son of a bitch!"

Mel jumps in her seat, knocking the table hard enough that her milk spills over the side of her mug. "Ma!"

"Well, he is." Ma slams the teacup to the table, tea pouring over the side. "If he was here, why, I'd... I'd..."

"Spill tea on him?" Mel snickers. She can't help it. The outrage on her mother's face closes up a crack inside of her. Her mother hasn't questioned that it happened. She believes her story. No question, no checking, not needing the whole tale.

The one time she'd tried to bring it up to her counselor at the VA, they'd asked her if she was drunk, and if she'd been drunk, is she sure she'd said no?

"Damn hot boiling tea, yes." The venom in her mother's voice is startling.

"I was drunk." Mel closes her eyes. She doesn't want to talk about that. She doesn't want her mother to know about the booze.

"So? Was he?"

Mel opens her eyes and shrugs. "And it wasn't...violent." He hadn't hit her or, well... he'd held her down, and it hadn't been fun and the penetration had hurt.

"Doesn't matter. Son of a bitch." Ma stands and stalks the kitchen.

There is humor in the situation. At least Mel thinks so and she laughs again.

"It isn't funny." Ma rounds on her, fists akimbo, anger flushing her cheeks with bright spots of color.

Mel stands, walking to her mother to put her arms around her. "I know." The tears start, falling hard.

"Oh, baby." Ma softens and wraps her arms around Mel, rocking her. "I never wanted that for you."

"I know."

"Your father didn't, either."

"I know that, too." And she does. No way her father wanted that to happen to her, even if he had disowned her.

"He was so worried. Followed all the news about Afghanistan and Iraq. Watched footage. I think he was looking for you."

Mel sniffs and rubs her nose in her mother's shoulder. She hadn't known that.

"He was a stubborn fool and I was too accommodating. I always thought he'd finally come around and call you. That if I gave him enough time, he'd figure it out." Ma pats her back and drags in a wet snuffle of her own. "Guess that makes me just as stubborn a fool as he was."

Nodding, Mel pulls back. "Do you want to know about the leg?"

"Do you want to tell me?"

"Yeah. That story will be a lot easier to get out." Mel catches a drop of tear with the fabric of her shirt on her shoulder.

"Okay. But let's have a cookie first." Ma leads the way to the table, pointing to the pile of crumbs Mel left behind. "You haven't even tasted them yet."

§

Afghanistan wasn't hot. It was dry and dusty, but the wind blew a cool breeze. Mel had expected heat, lots of heat.

The troops loaded into the transport vehicle, a long line of men and women leading from the back end of the C9 to the back of the first truck. Once full, the tailgate was raised and the lone shifted to the next truck. Each Marine or Soldier carried their rucksack and duffle.

Base camp looked temporary, Quonset huts and wooden buildings in straight lines, only the faintest lines of tires marking the roads. Marines marched to the edges, their uniforms blending into the never-ending beige.

"Girls in here and there." The Staff Sergeant that led the way pointed to a Quonset hut and then the next. "Drop your stuff on a bunk with nothing on it. You'll get your linens after chow."

Mel followed the other females Marines—five of them arrived today—into the first hut. With only three empty cots, Mel and another woman left, entering the next one, finding half a dozen cots with linens on them.

Dropping their rucksack and duffle on two cots, they left, meeting the other three outside. With no sign of the SSgt, they were lost; Mel had no idea where the chow hall was.

Stomach rumbling, she looked up and down the roadway. There were no signs indicating anything.

"Well, hello ladies." The Marine's insignia indicated he was a Gunney Sergeant. "Y'all lost?"

"Not if we're in Afghanistan." Mel narrowed her eyes at the man. He was tallish with blonde-brown hair, and eyes that squinted into the sun; lean, but then most Marines were, and he laughed.

It was a rumble that started in his chest and burst from his mouth.

Mel couldn't help but smile; the others were the same. Her stomach rumbled again, loud enough that everyone could hear it.

"C'mon and follow me. I'll show you around a little on our way to chow."

They followed, looking right and left whenever the Gunney pointed out a building or open space. A HUMVEE rattled past, troops visible in the back, bare heads slumped forward on drooping shoulders.

The chow hall was in the center of the base, equidistant from the barracks and the working areas. A row of conjoined Quonset huts sat just inside the tall barbed wire fence.

"That the motor pool and shop?" Mel pointed.

"Yeah." The Gunney looked her over. "Why?"

"I'm a mechanic. Figure that's where I'll be working."

"A mechanic?" He looked her over again.

"Yes."

"Huh." He looked back front and held the door open. "You don't look like a mechanic. Figured you were the new nurse."

"That would be me." The blonde at the head of their line answered, looking back at him.

"Oh. Okay."

The line for food snaked around the room. The odor of dust and sweat settled into the air, stronger than the aroma of the spaghetti and garlic bread that was being served as the main entree.

Mel took her place at the end of the line, behind the other women but in front of Gunney.

"Where you from?" He asked.

"Virginia. Tappahannock area."

"Where's that?"

"About an hour and half from Norfolk - on the river." Mel didn't want to talk about home. It reminded her of her parents and that she still hadn't talked to them. She'd been in for six years now, and still hadn't been back. It wasn't really home anymore.

"Home isn't near Twentynine Palms. That's where I've been stationed the past three years." And where her stuff was in storage--what little she'd accumulated. She'd lived on base, in the barracks, so it was mostly civilian clothes, books, and knick-knacks she hadn't been able to part with, most of it from vacations with Glenne.

Glenne was in Virginia Beach, with her surgeon husband. They had no kids yet, but they were working on that. Their house was near the Atlantic, and there had been discussion of Mel trying for orders close by, but that hadn't worked out.

"Got family in Twentynine Palms? Boyfriend?" They were at the stack of trays, still wet from the dishwasher, pools of water on the floor.

Mel picked up the top tray, tipping it to let the water drain. "No."

Gunney took the next tray, also letting the water drain off. He nodded toward the food. "Be careful when its goulash. I got some still raw one night."

Glancing back at him, Mel nodded. "I'll try to remember that."

"The spaghetti's okay—no meat in the sauce, though, and they put meatballs on if you want 'em." He grinned at the tall soldier serving the noodles. "It's always hit or miss when they get new guys in."

Mel took noodles and sauce, along with the meatballs. The server handed the plate over the top of the counter and she set it on the tray, waving her fingers to cool them from the too hot plate.

Gunney leaned close and tingles swept down her spine. "It's best to arrive early if you can. Once they're in rewash mode, everything is hot and wet."

Nodding, Mel swallowed and accepted a bowl of salad greens.

The girl that handed it to her smiled and nodded to the end. "Dressings and drinks are self-serve at the end."

"Thanks." Mel waited for the line to move, pouring Italian dressing over the limp salad and grabbing two glasses of iced tea.

"Want to sit with your friends?" Gunney paused behind her.

The other women had found a table, but there was no room for two other people at it.

"No. That's okay."

"Follow me." Gunney led her across the room to another table only half full. "It's easier to find a table early, too. Or late. But late might mean the food choices are scant. They tend to start running out of salad and veggies halfway through."

Sitting, Gunney dug into his meal, ceasing the conversation. Mel did the same, understanding that the goal is to eat and get out, not make chit chat. Others still had to eat, and they would need somewhere to sit.

After, Gunney continues showing her around the base, taking her to the motor pool, introducing her to the lead mechanic.

"Good to meet you, Manley. Didn't expect that until tomorrow morning after indoctrination." The man had graying hair and scarred hands.

"Gunney was nice enough to show me around."

"Yeah, he's great like that."

Gunney punched him in the arm, a good-joke gesture that makes the man laugh.

"Watch out for him, little girl." The man turned to lock the doors to the garage. "He's a ladies' man, that one."

Mel chafed at the little girl reference. She was twenty-eight for God's sake. She wasn't little and she wasn't a girl anymore. "Thanks."

The man walked away, whistling off key.

"He thinks he's funny. But he's easy to work for. You just need to prove yourself. If you can fix an engine, he's your best friend."

Nodding, Mel watched the man turn a corner.

"So, you ready to go back to your bed?" Gunney stood, hands resting on his hips, grinning.

"Careful, I'll start believing him." Mel smirked. "I need to grab linens and a pillow first. Where do I get those?"

"Follow me."

And she did.

**17**

## RECONNECTING

Brad and Chrissie wait beside their silver Honda. Chrissie is in a sundress and little white shrug and white open-toed pumps; Brad wears dress pants, shirt and tie. They look like they're going to church.

Mel feels underdressed. She's in jeans, boots, and un-tucked-but-pressed shirt: comfortable, her leg well hidden.

"Hi, Mel. It's good to have you home." Chrissie hugs her.

Surprised, Mel hugs her back before taking a step away.

"Let's go in. It's getting cool out here." Brad leads the way inside, to a large, bright room that resembles a hotel lobby. A large TV mounted to the wall shows the news; on mute, the words appear in the black boxes on the bottom of the screen. An unlit fireplace takes up one corner, and tables and chairs sit next to what looks like a coffee shop.

"Oh, this is nice." Ma looks around, smiling, her purse dangling from her clasped hands.

"Yeah." It also looks expensive. Windows along the back let in the light, and doors at either end of the wall lead out to a patio and small garden.

"Hello, hello. You must be the Manleys." A woman in a dress skirt, white blouse and vest strides across the room, hand outstretched. "I'm Vivian Maynard."

"Ms. Maynard." Brad accepts the handshake, as does Chrissie. Ma waves; Mel smiles. "I'm Brad Manley, this is my wife Chrissie. My mother, Veronica Manley called for the appointment to see an apartment."

"Of course, Mr. Manley."

"And this is my sister, Melanie."

Mel smiles but still doesn't extend a hand. Ms. Maynard reminds her of the administrator at the VA center. She doesn't want to get friendly.

"We have a ground floor one-bedroom unit, or a third-floor unit." Ms. Maynard smiles at Brad; it doesn't reach her eyes. "Which would you be interested in?"

Chrissie narrows her eyes. "You should be asking Ma that question. She's the one who wants to look at it."

It's said in a kind manner, but Mel suspects that Chrissie's demeanor could change in a heartbeat.

And for the first time Mel can ever remember, she feels like she could back her sister-in-law in that.

"Of course." The woman turns to Ma. "Mrs. Manley, do you have a preference?"

"Well, I don't need a first-floor apartment yet, but could I look at both?"

The woman's smile widens but her eyes remain flat. "Yes, of course. This way, please. We'll look at the ground-floor unit first."

Ma and Brad follow immediately behind Ms. Maynard, Chrissie and Mel bring up the rear.

"It pisses me off when someone does that." Chrissie's whisper is sharp and caustic.

"Does what?" Mel whispers back, keeping an eye on Ms. Maynard's back. It doesn't look like the woman can hear them or she's become adept at ignoring these types of side conversations.

"Ignores the real customer. My Aunt Tilly is in here, and according to my cousin, that woman did the same thing to her."

"And she still got an apartment here?"

"Everything else is really good. The on-call nurse is great and the doctor is available whenever they need him. It's just *her* that gets my groat up."

Mel nods.

At the door to the unit, Ms. Maynard turns and smiles, opening the door to let them precede her in.

Ma enters first, exclaiming over the space. It is a working size: the kitchenette opens to the four-seat dining area, a small hutch on the wall; the living area comfortable with two love seats making an ell to face the TV mounted in the corner; the bedroom next to the well-equipped bathroom.

"Ooh, there's a door out to the garden."

"Yes, all the ground-floor units have French doors to a small patio. The upper units have balconies." Ms. Maynard speaks from the door, letting them roam at will.

Mel opens the fridge and the microwave, checks out the stove and runs water in the sink. "It comes furnished?"

"Yes." Ms. Maynard doesn't smile.

Brad nods, checking the TV mount. "Cable?"

"Satellite. Comes with the monthly fee. As does the heating and cooling, water, electric...all utilities, including the internet and Wi-Fi."

Chrissie comes out of the bedroom. "Laundry?"

"Maids clean weekly; laundry pick up is part of their duties. They remake the bed and put out towels. If something is needed off schedule, it's just a phone call to ask."

"So," Mel turns and leans against the marble countertop, "the initial payment is for the share of the building—like buying a condo—then the monthly fee is for the services and utilities?"

"That's what I said."

"No, you didn't mention the initial purchase." Chrissie frowns at Ms. Maynard.

"My apologies."

"What about telephone?" Mel cranes her head. "I don't see a land line."

"Cell phones. If a resident needs a land line, they can use the phones in the office."

Mel isn't sure she likes that.

"It's been our experience that most families prefer the cell phone. Their parent only needs to remember a single number, and often the family pays the bill for that."

Ma frowns. "I don't have a cell phone."

"We can buy you one." Brad pats her shoulder. "But what do you think?"

"Is Maisie Williams here?" Ma asks Ms. Maynard.

Ms. Maynard's eyes grow big and she shifts her glasses on her nose. "I think she's on the overnight shopping trip to Potomac Mills."

"Oh." Ma's shoulders droop. "Where is her apartment?"

"She's on the second floor, I believe."

"And Tilly Smythe?"

"Third floor. Also on the Potomac Mills trip today."

Ma looks out the French doors, opening one to step outside. "I think I like this one. I don't need to look at the other one."

"Are you sure?" Mel frowns. She thinks her mother is making the decision too quick, and she worries there is a reason that she doesn't understand.

"Yes." Ma nods and strides back in, sliding the door behind her. "This is it."

"Well then," Ms. Maynard grins and claps her hands like there's a clap-on light somewhere that needs to be turned on, "we can start the paperwork."

"I have another question." Chrissie steps forward, raising a hand.

Ms. Maynard's lips tighten. "Yes?"

"How are residents notified if the monthly service fee increases? I'm sure at some point they will have to increase the fees, you know, when costs go up."

"Fees are locked in for a year at a time, calculated when the resident signs. They are given two months' notice of an increase before their anniversary date, and can, of course, move if they don't want to pay the increased fees."

"And these trips, they cost extra?"

"Yes. But activities are hosted on site that are free to residents."

Chrissie nods and looks out the window. "And residents can use the gardens whenever they want? To walk or entertain?"

"Within reason, yes. At holidays, we have a signup sheet to make sure everyone gets a fair shot."

"Ma?" Brad rests a hand on his mother's shoulder.

"Let's sign."

Ms. Maynard smiles again and leads the way to her office.

"Do you need me?" Mel glances into the small room. There are only two chairs in front of the heavy desk.

"No, dear." Ma kisses her on the cheek. "Why don't you and Chrissie get a coffee and catch up? Brad can do this with me."

Brad nods, kissing his wife and squeezing Mel's hand before he follows Ma into the office.

Chrissie dips her head in the direction of the coffee shop. "My treat."

Mel follows Chrissie and asks the barista for a medium coffee, black. Chrissie gets a Caramel Macchiato with skim milk. She shrugs at Mel. "I like my sugar."

They don't sit at a table, but take the to-go cups out to the garden. Benches and picnic tables and grills are tucked into nooks and crannies among the bushes and trees.

"It is nice here." Mel sips at the coffee, sucking in a cooling breath when it burns her tongue

"Yeah." Chrissie sips her beverage with caution. "I'm waiting for the catch. My aunt was caught off guard by the rise in fees the first year."

"Was it a decent increase?"

"No, but she's on a fixed income. My cousin has to supplement some months. Probably more in the future."

"Okay." Mel thinks her coffee is too weak, but takes another sip anyway.

"Bleah." Chrissie makes a face. "Is there any coffee in your cup? I think this is straight milk."

"I think they used coffee water instead of the real thing." They find a nearby trash can so they dump their drinks. Mel considers her sister-in-law: Chrissie's hair is big—curly—just as it had been in high school, though not as blonde. And she doesn't wear as much makeup as back then, nor is she as tanned.

"Brad worried about you all the time. He hated that your dad wouldn't contact you. Brad tried to get your number once, but he couldn't because he was just your brother and nothing had happened to your parents."

Mel doesn't know what to say. She'd never realized anyone from her family had tried to call. "I guess I should have called Brad."

"You called your parents."

"Yeah."

"Your mom talked about that for a month after it happened. Gave your dad the cold shoulder big time. He was even making his own meals. He wouldn't back down, though, and she eventually caved in."

They reach the end of the garden, a tall brick wall with vines growing along the top and spilling over the side.

"What's on the other side?"

"The elementary school."

"Cool."

"Yeah. It's pretty safe here, I think." Chrissie pivots and walks back. "The kids can visit after school some days if your mom wants."

Mel laughs. "She'll want. That might be one of the reasons she wants to move here."

"That, and Maisie's been talking it up since she got her apartment. Tilly, too." Chrissie stops. "Mel?"

"Yeah?" Mel turns to face her.

"I'm glad you're back."

Mel stares a moment. Chrissie looks like she wants to cry; her eyes are pink-rimmed and her cheeks flushed.

"I think I'm glad to be back, too." She manages to speak the words before her throat closes.

Chrissie licks her lips. "I heard Brad and your mom on the phone, talking about your leg. Are you okay?"

Shifting, Mel looks down at the hidden prosthetic. "Yeah. Not perfect, not whole, but I'm getting better."

"Will you be here at Thanksgiving?"

She usually goes to Glenne's when she's stateside. "I haven't thought that far ahead yet." But she should. Think about it. It was only a month away now. Maybe she could invite Glenne and Rick up here?

"Your mom usually comes to the house, and my parents. Last year my sister and her kids came, too. Brad deep fries the turkey, or at least he has the last few years. And everyone brings something. My mom always brings pie, and your mom always brings her rolls. Extra because everyone loves them so much."

"If I'm here, I'll be there."

"If you're with Ozzie's family, I'll understand."

"Ozzie's? Why would I be with him?" Mel stares at the pattern of a leaf. Her cheeks heat, no matter how hard she tries to keep it from happening.

Chrissie snorts. "Please. Everyone knows he's yours. If you'd been a little more observant in high school, you might have had him then."

"What?" Mel blinks, refocusing on her sister's grinning face.

"He's always been soft for you, Mel. You were younger, though, so he kept his distance. Then, you joined the Marines and he wound up married to the dingbat."

"Dingbat?" Mel laughs, but it's weak. She needs to suck air into her lungs.

"That's what I call her. Didn't recognize the good thing she had and blew it. Waste of a woman, really. Ozzie deserves much better—like you."

"I might not be that much better for him." Mel trudges toward the apartment building.

Chrissie jogs to catch up. "Yes, you are. He smiles all the time now. For the last couple of years, the only time anyone saw him smile was when he was with his kids."

"I'm missing part of my leg."

"He doesn't seem to care. And truth be told, if I hadn't known, I never would have realized. Your limp isn't that bad."

"Sometimes it is."

"We're all a little dented, Mel. Hell, I can clear a room in half a heartbeat if I eat cheese or drink milk. I have to down half a box of Lactaid for the kids' birthday parties so I can have a little ice cream with their cake. And Brad's already on cholesterol and blood pressure meds."

Mel jerks her head around at Chrissie. She never expected to have this type of conversation with her. She's never understood Brad's attraction, but now, she thinks she might.

"And not just physically. Even Ozzie is a little broken. And I couldn't tell you all the times Brad and I have fought and decided that was the end of it, only to make up and try again. Life is ugly and mean, and it's up to us to put the paint on it."

Snickering, Mel stumbles.

Chrissie catches her and laughs with her.

"Hey!" Brad calls from the main patio. "We're done and Ma's ready for lunch!"

"We'll be right there." Chrissie calls back. "We're participating in a girl-bonding ritual."

Brad stares a moment before shaking his head and retreating inside.

"I love him."

Mel sighs. "Me, too. But not the same way, you know..."

Giggling, feeling light inside, Mel links arms with her sister-in-law's and they match step all the way to the doors.

§

Mel and Gunney got along from day one. They laughed at the same jokes, mock battled for the last piece of the same flavor pie because it was their favorite—even found out they got the same score on the ASVAB.

Best mates in battle.

Gunney had her back. She knew that.

And she had his.

"Hey, I'm gonna go take a smoke break with the Adj. Cover for me, eh?" Gunney rapped the table in the garage office.

"When did smoking go against regs?" Mel pulled the schematics down for the radio wiring in a HUMVEE.

"It ain't. As long as its straight tobacco." Gunney's guffaw remained hanging in the room even after he'd left out the side door.

Mel shrugged and set the schematics on the desk. She needed to figure out why the radio kept cutting out every time one of the vehicles hit a bump. The radio tested fine, so it had to be something in the connections to the battery—and that was her problem, not the radiomen or the radio techs.

An hour later, having traced the power source to the proper fuse box and found it loose in its bracket, Mel was happy that she'd done her job.

"Hey, you seen Gunney?" It was the Adjutant, a First Lieutenant a month out from Basic School.

"Not since he went for his smoke."

The Adjutant blinked and shuffled. "He didn't come back here?" He straightened and cleared his throat.

Ah, shit. What was Gunney supposed to do?

"Not that I saw." Mel closed the access panel to the fuse box. "But then, I've had my head in this HUMVEE all afternoon. He probably dropped in and I didn't notice."

The young officer nodded and swallowed. "If he comes in, can you tell him I need to see him?"

Mel nodded. "Sure. Should I look for him?"

"No, no. I'm sure it was a misunderstanding." And the Adj pivoted like he was in boot camp and marched away.

A misunderstanding?

Sighing, Mel secured the access hatches on the HUMVEE and marked its paperwork as "work completed", then logged into the computer to write up what she'd done and why. She was skimming over what she'd typed when Gunney sauntered in.

"Hey." He leaned his arms on the back of a chair by the desk.

"Hey yourself. The Adj was by looking for you."

Gunney jerked and straightened. "What did you tell him?"

"Nothing. What could I tell him?"

"That I was off in Supply looking for his fucking pins."

Mel looked up from the screen for a moment, hit the return key on the keyboard to submit her form and leaned on the desk. "I could have told him that, if I'd known to tell him that."

"Jeezus, Manley!"

"I told him I'd been under the hood of the HUMVEE all afternoon and that you'd likely left me alone to fix it. Again—if I don't know the cover, I can't lie for you."

"He's going to expect me to have those fucking pins."

Mel shook her head and turned back to the computer. "Sorry, I didn't know what to tell him."

"I suppose you just stammered it out, like you didn't know what to say?"

"I'm not stupid, Gunney. Of course not." You'd think she'd never covered for him before.

She didn't bother asking where he'd been. He'd probably gotten more of whatever he'd been smoking with the Adjutant and spent the afternoon in a haze of smoke. Glancing over his sneering face, she noted his pink-rimmed watery eyes and red nose. Oh yeah. He was half-way to high or better.

Not that she blamed him. He'd been extended here. The last place on earth anyone would want their tour of duty extended.

"I'm sure it's fine. It's just the Adj." Mel stretched in her chair and stood up, switching off the monitor. They never shut off the computer; if they did, or it powered off for some reason, it took almost an hour to power back up. "Go see him and tell him you couldn't find the pins."

"Colonel won't like that."

Mel couldn't help her snicker. "Then someone should have been looking for the damn pins."

"Come help me." Gunney stood and sauntered forward, running one finger along her temple and leaning close to nuzzle the soft flesh at her ear. "You know you want to."

"No, I don't want to go looking for some damn pins. But I will. To save your ass."

Gunney grinned. "And it's a very fine ass." He spun around and led the way out.

It was a nice ass, high and tight, looking fine in the dusty camouflage trousers. Gunney's entire body was nothing but tight muscle.

Best thing was, once they'd found the pins, she'd get to see it close up.

§

"I don't think that truck has ever sounded that smooth." Gary stands next to the raised hood of the Ford, hands on his hips, nodding to the thrumming beat of the engine.

"Oh, I'm sure it did once." A rush of pride hits Mel. She's fixed Ma's truck, under budget and in a shorter time than planned.

"Maybe when it was fresh off the line." The mechanic pats Mel on the shoulder. "Hate to say it Mel, but your dad didn't know much about engines."

"He knew enough to bring it here to get fixed, didn't he?"

"Well, yeah." Gary rubs a greasy hand at the back of neck. "But usually it was almost too far gone when it got here, and Jackson Manley never liked spending much to fix it."

Mel chuckles. "He liked keeping his money. Liked to make stuff last as long as he could."

Hell, her dad had tinkered and patched the old dishwasher at the farm for twenty years, and the washing machine for twenty-five. When he'd finally decided to replace them, the new machines had been birthday and Christmas presents for Ma. And when the toilet on the first floor had started flushing on its own, they'd had to turn the water valve off after every use because he'd refused to call the plumber out.

Shaking his head, Gary drops the hood over the humming engine and presses it down to catch the latch. "He could squeeze the last drop of juice out of a watermelon."

"Did you know he served? In the Army?"

Gary freezes then turns, face pale. "No, Mel. I didn't."

Mel nods, not sure she should be telling Gary her family secrets. Her father and Gary had been friends. Had talked and hung out at school functions, watching their respective children perform, whether it be sport or acting or singing.

"Don't think anyone in town knew that."

"I didn't until I came home this time and Ma showed me his stuff." Mel reaches in and turns the truck's engine off. "It was hidden up in the attic."

"Why didn't he tell anyone?"

Mel shrugs. "Note sure."

Maybe that's why she's telling Gary. Maybe she hopes that Gary knows, not everything but something; she'd be happy if he could give just a hint at why.

"I guess," Mel swallows gathering tears, "I was hoping you knew and could tell me something about that."

"Some people don't like to talk about their service time. It isn't all good stuff." Something dark flashes across the man's face.

Mel snorts. "You don't have to tell me that."

"Figured I didn't." Gary wipes his hands on a rag and drops it in a refuse bin. "You haven't said much about your time in."

Staying silent, Mel stares into the truck cab, at the worn seats and stained carpet, the cracking vinyl dash, leaning her forehead against the cool metal of the door.

"I'm here if you ever want to talk. I may know more about that than you know, too." Gary pats her on the shoulder again and passes into the office. "I'm sorry I don't know more about Jackson's service. I'd tell you if I knew something. You know that, right?"

"Yeah." Mel straightens and turns around, pasting a wide grin on her face. She knocks her knuckles on the closed hood. "Least I got the truck running in time to help Ma move."

"There is that." Gary's voice is muffled by distance and the office walls. "When's she moving?"

"She's been packing all week." Mel walks into the office, standing in the door to look for Gary. She can hear him but can't see him. "Brad has Saturday off, so we're going to load up as many vehicles as we can and try to do it in one day."

"Vehicles?" Gary pops up over the counter, clipboard in hand.

"Well, the truck, his car, and the station wagon Chrissie drives the kids around in. I think it belongs to her parents."

"What is she moving? I thought those apartments were furnished?"

Mel leans against the counter, happy the discomfit of the previous subject is behind her. "It is. But she's taking a bunch of knickknacks and all her clothes and some of the smaller furniture she got from her mother. A little antique table that was in her bedroom, and all her pictures. She's packed it all up so there's more paper in the box than anything else."

Gary shakes his head and writes something on the papers on the clipboard. "You ready to start a job?"

Mel blinks. "That's still on?" She's wondered. They'd talked about it; her rates, the hours, no benefits—not that she needed any, she had the VA. They've also fought about how to care for the tools and what she needed to do to fix the truck.

"Yup."

Blinking, Mel straightens, hands pressing flat on the countertop. "You sure?"

"Yup. I need a good mechanic. Not always full-time work, and sometimes it's more than full time, but-" He shrugs and stares her square on. "We did talk about this."

Mel swallows.

Gary smirks. "If you want, I can make it temporary."

"That would probably be for the best, at least for now." Mal taps her fingers on the countertop and laughs. "I get Saturday, off. Right? I mean, Ma would be right pissed off if I couldn't help her move."

"Yeah," Gary snickers and hangs the clipboard on a peg beside the door, "I suppose you can have Saturday off."

"Monday morning, then? Half-past seven so I can take care of the animals?"

"Make it nine. That way I'll have enough coffee in me to handle your sass and stubborn-as-a-mule mouth."

§

Colonel Benton's bellow made everyone in the motor pool jump; tools hit the dirt, some clanging against the metal engine compartments on the way down.

"Sergeant Manley!"

Mel swallowed and set the wrench still in her hand on the workbench and marched forward, taking a deep breath to keep her voice from shaking. It didn't work. "Ye-es, Sir? I'm Manley. But it's-"

The Colonel squinted his eyes and looked her up and down. "Get over here." He pointed at the ground in front of him.

She wiped sweaty palms down her camo-covered thighs and obeyed. What had she done now? The front office clerk—a Staff Sergeant—and the Colonel's aide—a 1st Lieutenant—smirked and shuffled their feet. The Staff Sergeant held something behind his back, but she couldn't tell what it was.

Once she was standing two feet before the Colonel. Mel straightened but didn't salute—she wasn't wearing her cover. Should she anyway?

The Colonel raised his hand to his forehead, so she jerked his hand up, smearing grease over her temple.

The Staff Sergeant handed a red folder to the 1st Lieutenant, who flipped it open and started reading:

"To all those who see these present, greeting:

Know Ye, that reposing special trust and confidence in the fidelity and abilities of Melanie M. Manley, I do appoint this Marine a Staff Sergeant in the United States Marine Corps to rank as such from the first day of June, two thousand fifteen.

This appointee will therefore carefully and diligently discharge the duties of the grade to which appointed by doing and performing all manner of things thereunto pertaining. And I do strictly charge and require all personnel of lesser grade to render obedience to appropriate orders. And this appointee is to observe and follow such orders and directions as may be given from time to time by Superiors acting according to the rules and articles governing the discipline of the Armed Forces of the United States of America.

Given under my hand at Kabul, Afghanistan, 1st Marine Division this first day of June, in the year of our Lord two thousand seventeen—signed, General A. J. Smith, USMC.

Colonel Benton grinned at Mel, dropped his hand and handed her the folder, holding out one hand to shake hers.

Silent—she couldn't find the words to say anything intelligent—she shook his hand and took the folder, snapping back to attention to salute once again.

"Staff Sergeant," the motor pool Gunnery Sergeant tapped her shoulder, "you are out of uniform regs."

"What?" Mel spun to look at him.

He poked the Sergeant insignia on her arm. "Better change that before I write you up."

Mel blinked.

Gunney shook his head and barked out a laugh. "I'm joking, Marine. It's okay. Wearing the correct rank tomorrow will be fine."

The front office clerk laughed and reached back into the command Jeep, pulling out a crisp uniform shirt, the insignia of Staff Sergeant freshly sewn on the arm. "Here," he handed it to Mel, "this will get you started."

The rest of the motor pool erupted in applause and cheers.

The Gunnery Sergeant sighed. "You know what this is for?"

Mel shook her head, her glance darting from his face, to the Colonel's, to the clerk and aide's. "No, Sir. I don't."

The Colonel cleared his throat and the motor pool leader took a step back. "Staff Sergeant Manley, do you remember when all those transports came in and needed to get repaired to get back out in the field?"

She nodded. There had been seven, one having run over an IED, the debris and shrapnel from the road-side bomb damaging all the follow vehicles.

"You," he pointed at her, then poked her shoulder, "are why our Marines got back out as soon as they did, with transports fully repaired and ready to support the mission. You had to scavenge parts—some from the vehicles that had just come in—but we completed the mission, got back out there fighting the fight, because of you and your leadership. BZ Marine." And he clapped a hand to her shoulder, shaking her a little.

When the small entourage of brass had left, Mel reread the citation and rubbed a thumb over sleeve of the new shirt. She couldn't believe it.

Someone snorted; someone else guffawed.

The Gunnery Sergeant spun around. "Someone got a problem?"

"Yeah," a new mechanic stepped forward, "I do. How come she gets promoted, just like that?"

"You heard the Colonel." The NCO narrowed his gaze. "She rose above and beyond."

"Sure it ain't 'cause she's fucking someone in the front office?"

The Marine standing next to speaker slugged him in the arm. "Shut the fuck up. Manley don't work like that."

"Hey, I've been working my ass off and I'm still a Lance Corporal."

"Yup." The slugger nodded. "And stood around like a baby with his finger up his nose when all that work came in. But Manley over here took stock of it all and got to work."

"I worked on them, too."

"We all worked on them." The Gunnery Sergeant got in the Lance Corporal's face. "Even me, when Manley called me in to help. But Manley's the one who took charge and evaluated them and made a plan of action that got enough of them back up and running that we got the mission done. That," he sniffed, "*boy*," he spat the word, "is what makes a Marine. You might be in the wrong service if you think you get ahead just by doing your job."

Mel gritted her teeth. She wanted to defend herself, but let her fellow Marines do it for her. It was hard, keeping her mouth shut, but she knew that her words wouldn't be heard, and could make everything worse.

# 18

## NOT AN EMBED

Mel hates the news, especially despises the people delivering it. Sitting behind a fake desk in a fake room, in pretty fake clothes, no dirt on their fake faces, hair combed, makeup perfect, talking about the front lines like it isn't an emotional rollercoaster.

Their voices are steady, their mouths an eternal upturned half-smile, their eyes a coy come-on to induce regular folks to keep watching. Their words upbeat, like death isn't the most somber thing to talk about.

Like people weren't dying.

Not that ending a war would be easy, but it would certainly be less bloody. Les traumatic. Less devastating.

She punches the mute button on the TV remote, staring at the moving mouths, not caring that she can't hear what they are saying. It's always the same: Americans are dead; insurgents are dead. Civilians are dead, too: men, women, children, their pet dogs. All a bloody mess while leaders on both sides sit in their high towers, safe, sound, under no threat, placing orders that will make people die like their running through a drive thru.

Groaning, she turns the TV off, the static discharge the only sound. A rasp on her frayed nerves.

Her heart beats, hard and fast. It's pumping in her ears. Placing her hand on her chest, she tries to keep it in, keep it under control—but she can't.

She can see the blood—lots of it, covering faces and arms and hands, not all of it attached—and she gags.

Slapping her head with her palms, she tries to knock the images away. But they remain steadfast, determined to make her pay.

After all, she is alive and well and no longer on the front line.

Staggering to her feet, she trips to the kitchen, past the big scarred table that looks like a mortuary slab in that moment, the lights off, only the moon sharing its grey light; out to the hall, shoving her shaking leg into the closest muck boots, stumbling out the door.

She wants to scream, and she opens her mouth, but no sound comes out. It's trapped inside, building, so that she thinks she might explode.

The Miata's trunk has what she needs. Tapping the unlock button twice, the lid pops open. Inside, beneath an old blanket and behind a couple of boxes of old papers, is the bin where she's hidden her stash.

Reaching in, blind, not caring what she pulls out, she tugs the foil off the cover: it's a twist cap. Easy-peasy.

Swallowing half the bottle in one go, she doesn't bother tasting it. All she needs is the feeling it will bring—or rather the absence of feeling she would have in its aftermath. The void inside empty and vacant, cleansed but filthy.

Emitting a keening, high-pitched moan, she finishes the bottle and tosses the empty glass back in the trunk. She reaches for a second bottle; another twist-off cap. She'd been smarted with this last purchase. Made it easy on herself.

Turning, she sinks to the ground, not caring it's damp, the cold seeping through the denim on her backside to chill her skin, the stones and pebbles hard and unforgiving.

She doesn't deserve forgiveness.

§

An hour later, maybe two, she's in bed.

It had taken three tries to make it upstairs to her bedroom, and she'd staggered into the bathroom to vomit in the toilet first, but she'd made it, ripping herself out of her clothes, jerking off the prosthetic to throw it in the corner before collapsing on the bed.

Not asleep but nearly passed out when her mother gets home from her church meeting. She's downstairs, accompanied by another voice, also older, also feminine.

Grabbing her pillow, she covers her head, pressing it to her ears. She doesn't want to hear their laughter. Not now. Maybe not ever again.

It doesn't last long. Both women are tired, and the other one needs to drive back home. Their goodbyes become muted by distance, but the sounds echo in Mel's ears.

The stairs creak with each of her mother's footsteps.

Mel grits her teeth, willing herself to stay still in bed, to look relaxed under her sheet, asleep, oblivious. Her mother is going to look in on her.

No light, just the slightly louder rasp of breath of an older woman who has walked up a flight of stairs, then the door closing and another opening.

And oblivion comes for real.

# 19

## HANGOVER

Mel's head pounds before she wakes up, the pain rattling her brain into awareness. She lays in bed a moment, reveling in the insistent ache—it means she hadn't died last night.

A part of her had wanted to—she hates those memories, worse when they aren't as a dream, but truly a memory. She remembers drinking, too, and wonders if Ma realizes she'd gotten drunk last night.

Rolling over, her stomach heaving so that her throat burns with stomach acid, Mel groans and hates the world. She knows it's her own fault, that she can't blame anyone else, that she has to decide to not let the alcohol control her.

That's what her counselor says, and the therapist, and her medical doctor. It isn't as easy as they like to make her think.

Standing, she makes it to the hall and the bathroom, rinsing her mouth and brushing her teeth. There is Advil in the medicine cabinet, so she takes two, swallowing them down with a handful of tap water.

"Mel? You up?" Ma's voice is bright and jolly. They're supposed to finish moving her into her apartment today.

She opens the bathroom door and hollers out. "Yeah. Give me a couple minutes and I'll be down."

"Want coffee?"

The thought of coffee makes her stomach heave, more acid swelling up her throat. "No. Maybe some milk."

"You okay?"

"Let's just say I'm awake and leave it at that, okay?"

There is a pause of silence and something about it catches Mel's attention. There is no sound from the kitchen—no clang of pot or rush of water, no thuck as the fridge is opened to retrieve the milk.

"Ozzie called this morning."

*Ozzie.* Mel closes her eyes and lets her head hang from her neck. Should she call him back? Did he realize what had happened to her yesterday? If anyone would, it would be him.

"What did he say?"

"Wondered how you were. If you were up yet." The sound of coffee being poured and the slap of a milk jug contacting a flat surface amke it to her ears.

"Okay, I'll call him after breakfast."

"No need. I invited him over since he hadn't gone into work yet."

Mel takes in a quick, sharp breath. Ozzie is coming. He'll see her and realize she'd gotten drunk last night. And is hung over now.

Damn.

Closing the bathroom door, Mel spends extra time trying to erase the remaining signs of alcohol in her system. In the end, the result is the same. She looks hung over.

And Ozzie will be able to tell.

His voice rises up the stairs, laughing and talking with her mother, complimenting the pancakes, the hashbrowns, the eggs, and bacon. Her mother has gone all out this morning.

Clomping down the stairs, Mel steals herself for the look she expects to get from Ozzie--the pity, the disdain--and the one from her mother--the sly wink and nudge about the fact that Ozzie had called and come over.

The table is set and waiting, a talk glass of milk next to her plate sending her stomach into unexpected cramps. Maybe milk is not the beverage of choice after all.

Mel sits at her regular place, Ozzie sitting to her left.

"Good morning." Ozzie's voice is jubilant, and echoes in her brain.

"Morning." She eyes the milk, wondering if the threats from her stomach are real or just bluffs.

"Are you sure you don't want coffee, hon?" Ma stands at the counter and transfers the bacon from a paper towel, where it's been losing the grease, to a clean plate for the table.

"Yeah, the milk is enough." It doesn't matter about the milk--or the coffee--she would make double-certain everything stayed down. "Everything smells great."

"Thank you." Once the bacon is on the table, Ma takes her place and sips her coffee. "I did wonder. You were up late last night."

Mel takes in a noisy breath. "Yeah. I couldn't fall asleep."

"You okay?" Ozzie has three pancakes on his plate, butter melting into their warmth, syrup dripping over the edges. He is definitely onboard with the big breakfast.

"Just tired." She takes a couple pancakes of her own and liberally pours the syrup over. "Yesterday's incident was, let's say, disturbing." Why bother denying it? Might as well start the conversation herself.

Ozzie selected a couple slices of bacon. "It was disturbing for me, too. Downed a whole six-pack of beer before I realized what I was doing and stopped."

Setting her fork down, Mel stared at her plate, the oozing syrup looking decidedly reddish in her mind. "At least you stopped."

"What?" Ma's coffee mug slammed to the table. "Mel?"

"There are three empty bottles of wine in the bottom of the recycle bin." She kept her gaze on her plate, watching the syrup bead on the plate, then the beads combine into a small puddle of sugar.

Ozzie put a gentle hand on her arm. "How you doing this morning?"

Mel shrugs, but not hard enough to dislodge his hand. It is warm, a comfort she hadn't expected. "After the booze, I slept without any nightmares."

"That why you drank?"

"Yeah." Mel picks up her fork in her right hand, not moving her left where Ozzie's hand still rests. She cuts the tines into the pancakes. "I think that's why I ever get drunk. So I can sleep through the night."

"Makes the morning suck." Ozzie squeezes his hand, pressing the warmth farther into her skin.

"Really, no worse than if I hadn't slept."

"Mel?" Ma's voice is low, rusty like she hadn't used it for a while.

Mel looks up, noting the watery eyes, the pale cheeks. "It's okay, Ma. I usually make sure I can't find anything to drink."

"Where did the wine come from?"

"I stopped by the ABC store on the way home yesterday. There are two more in my trunk."

"What are you going to do with those?" Ozzie leans forward to catch her gaze.

"Dump them down the toilet."

"Okay." Ozzie lets go of her arm and her skin chills.

Not 'good'. Not 'smart move'. Just 'okay.'

"Maybe you should talk to someone." Ma's hands are in her lap.

"Yeah. Talk to someone." Mel shoves the piece of pancake into her mouth.

"I mean-"

The swallow almost sticks in her throat, but Mel gets it down. "I know, Ma." She puts her fork down and rubs over her eyes, smearing tears over her cheeks. "Talking doesn't help. I've tried that. I've tried talking, I've tried group counseling. I've tried twelve-step. I've tried everything the VA offers, but it hasn't helped."

"Time helps." Ozzie stares at Ma. "Home helps."

Ma nods and picks up her own fork, picking at the hash browns and eggs on her plate.

The therapist's name was Amanda; Mel couldn't remember her last name. She made them sit in a circle, in hard plastic chairs, in the center of the large room.

Six veterans, one with a missing leg, another older than dirt. One said he'd been in the Navy, one from the Army, the others were all Marines.

Mel was the only female, except for the therapist.

They were in the basement recreation room of a church, either Baptist or Methodist—Mel knew it ended with an -ist. The piano in the corner wasan old baby grand, the top worn; it was probably donated by someone who'd gotten abrand new one and needed the tax write-off.

During the day, the open room served as a day care, evidenced by the preschool toys, toddler cots, and tiny chairs in another corner.

"So," her cheery, over-bright voice echoed in the rafters, "how are we doing tonight?"

The circle grunted as one, even Mel. How did she expect them to be? It had been a week since their last session, a week of nightmares and booze and binge eating. Mel had gained five pounds in two weeks.

"Come on, guys, I need some real answers." Amanda grinned, a little too toothy for Mel.

"I fucking sucked." The language didn't surprise Mel; she'd heard a lot worse and expected to hear more tonight, though it coming from the oldest in the room was unsettling. It was like hearing your grandfather swear.

"Mr. Michael, remember your language." Amanda wagged a finger.

"I'm sure he remembers his fucking language. I'm sure he remembers a whole fucking lot more than most of us." It is the other Marine with a leg missing.

Amanda take a breath but keeps her smile. "I want us to concentrate on our successes this week. who wants to share?"

The therapist looked to be all of 18, though she must be older to have a degree and have been certified to hold these sessions. Even the VA had standards.

"Melanie?"

"It's just Mel." Why couldn't the diphead remember she didn't like her full name? "And I don't think I have anything to share."

"Oh, I'm sure you do." Amanda nodded and smiled harder.

"Well, I'm still here. Haven't jumped out a window yet. Is that considered a success?"

Everyone but Amanda laughed.

"Nah, Mel. It's still a failure 'cause you thought about jumping." It was the Army guy, who winks at her. He had a tattoo on both forearms; one new enough the skin was still pink around the ink.

"That's not how it works." Amanda raised a hand. "We celebrate the little successes as well as the big ones."

"Yeah, but a little failure's as bad as the big one." It's the old one-legged-one-armed Marine again, and the old guy snorts out a gust of laughter.

Amanda's face turned pink. "That not true. We need to recognize the little failures—like thinking of jumping. We need to focus on positive thoughts all the time."

"I am positive that I am going to get drunk tonight." The sailor stood and stretched. "Look, I appreciate you trying, but this ain't working for me."

"That's not what I mean." Amanda stood, too, the flush extending down her neck. "And you need to stay."

"Look lady, I don't need to do anything." The sailor turned his back, flipping the bird at the therapist at the door. "See you in the obits."

The remaining five patients sat quiet. Amanda stood, lips pursed, bright spots of color still in her cheeks. "Anyone else want to leave?"

The soldier raised a hand. "I don't want to be here. That the same thing?"

"Why don't you want to be here?"

"I don't like talking to you about what happened. You can't relate to it."

"I'm a certified therapist. I work for the VA." She flails her arms and paces.

"But you've never been a soldier. Or a marine or a sailor. There is no way you understand what I went through. What any of us in here went through." He jumped from his chair, striding to the door. At least he didn't flip the bird on the way out.

"Melanie?"

"Maybe I'd stay if you could remember my name." Mel stood, waiting to see if the woman called her Mel. She didn't, so Mel left, not angry, just disappointed.

# 20

## MUSTANG GUNNY

The old mustang gleams in the sun, and Mel grins. It's a beauty from the early 70s—sleek with narrow fenders and fat tires in the back. The paint isn't an original color, but a newer metallic. Someone's spent a lot of time and money to keep it looking new.

The engine revs, then cuts off and the driver door opens. Gunney steps out, in board shorts and a loose t-shirt, his hair a little longer on top but still close on his neck. It's long enough she can tell the gray from the gold.

No fucking way.

Mel backs away from the window, praying he hasn't seen her.

He pulls his aviator shades from his face and squints at the Miata. She'd parked it in the shade to keep it cooler. She'd damn near burnt the back of her thighs off after visiting her mother at her new apartment. She'd suggested Ma take a garage unit in the long building behind the apartments, as well as the one-bedroom.

Brad and Chrissie are helping her unpack today. Mel plans to go over this evening, after work—after finishing two oil changes and a carburetor cleaning—to help her put stuff away.

Shit a bull patty.

Spinning away, Mel sprints for the bathroom, opening the door and slamming it behind her. She rams the lock in place and sits on the closed toilet. Shit! What is he doing here?

"Mel, you okay?" It's Delta. From the volume of her voice, she must be pressing her face against the door.

"Fine." The word croaks out, low and raspy. It sounds like her voice in the morning after a drunken binge at midnight. She hopes the other woman has heard her.

The bell above the office door rings and soft footsteps trail in the direction of the office.

"Can I help you?" Mel can hear the smile in Delta's voice.

"I was wondering about the black Miata." Gunney's voice is all country-boy charm with a Tennessee accent. Mel cringes inside. There is no way Delta won't melt under it. He's too good-old-boy suave.

"Oh, it isn't for sale. One of our mechanics owns it." Mel imagines Delta leaning over the counter and batting her lashes at Gunney.

"Is your mechanic in?"

"Who's asking?" Gary's voice cuts across the conversation and reverberates through the bathroom door. He must have heard the question from the shop bay and come in.

"A friend."

"You ain't a friend of mine. He a friend of yours, Delta?"

"No." Her voice turns cool.

"I'm a friend of the Miata owner." Gunney clears his voice and Mel imagines him standing in the door, that solid blue gaze sweeping from Gary to Delta and back—unless he's fixated it on Delta and her cleavage.

"If you're a friend, how come you had to ask about it?"

"Look, I'm a vet-"

"So what? So am I. Served in 'nam. Got lots of medals to prove it."

Gary had served in Vietnam? Mel didn't think he was old enough to have served over there. Of course, she'd never thought about how old Gary might be. Just that he was old. Old enough to have known her as a kid, and her parents and this whole town.

Oh, hell. He was her dad's age, and her dad had served in Vietnam.

You can learn a lot eavesdropping in bathrooms.

The silence crawls under the locked door and fills the tiny room. It nearly suffocates Mel, and she drags in a hot, quiet breath. Tears leak out her eyes, and she swipes at them with her fingers, smearing old engine grease over her cheeks.

"Is Mel here?" Gunney's voice sounds pissed.

"Nope." Gary's sounds angry.

"Is that her car?"

"You said you know the owner. Is it?"

"I have a friend who can run the plates."

"I'm pretty sure that's illegal."

"Just tell me if Mel's here."

"She isn't." This time, it's Delta who speaks. Mel is surprised. After all, she's sitting right here in the toilet and Delta knows it. "Ozzie picked her up earlier."

Damn, why did she have to bring Ozzie into it?

"Ozzie." Gunney snorts. "What is he, an eighty-year-old cab driver?"

"He's our fire chief." Gary joins back in.

"Fire chief?"

"Yup."

"What? Is Mel volunteering or something? I heard she's only got one leg now."

"Or something." Delta again—and she's starting to sound like Gary. What is Gunney doing? He usually has a way with women that makes them swoon when he breathed. Granted, that wouldn't work as well on Gary, but she's seen him con an officer into letting him off when the officer had caught him red-handed with his fingers in the proverbial goody jar.

The door slams, the bell ringing hard and smacking the frame. Mel shudders on the toilet, taking in a deep breath that does nothing to steady her or stop her hands from shaking.

Someone knocks. "Hey. It's Delta."

Mel stretches out a hand and unlocks the door, expecting Delta to open it and speak to her.

Instead, the other woman slides into the small room, closing and relocking the door behind her. "Oh, sweetie."

Sniffing, Mel runs a sleeve over her nose. "I probably look like shit that's been run over."

Delta remains silent, standing by the door, a look of empathy and understanding fixed on her face. But when the sobbing starts, she kneels and wraps her arms around Mel and rocks with her.

§

She had to be quiet. If someone heard her, they'd ask why. And she couldn't explain to anyone why she was crying. She wasn't even sure herself.

There was no sense in it. Nothing could be done now. If she told—and who would believe her anyway, she'd have to prove it and she couldn't now—it wouldn't just be Gunney's career on the chopping block, but her own, as well. The whole affair would come out.

And then some.

All those other girls. They would be called out, too.

And then there was the booze. She'd been drunk. Maybe she'd said yes, maybe she'd said no. She could only remember half of it anyway.

Gunney would say it was consensual. After all, they'd been doing it for months. She was just disgruntled and lying because she'd found out she wasn't the only one.

She knew how that worked. She'd seen it. Even stateside, it was word against word, and they never believed the victim.

When Mel was in high school, a woman in Richmond who'd been raped by a man on a date went to the police, and the media had only dragged her name through the sewers, relating stories of how many boyfriends she'd had and how many times she'd had sex and that she liked to frequent the clubs and bars on ladies' nights. Like that somehow made her a bad person. Made what happened her fault.

No mention of the number of girls he'd dated or how many he'd had sex with or that he also like to drink and party.

He'd gotten nothing—no fine, no time in jail—he didn't even have to register as a sex offender.

And she'd moved away to start her life somewhere else, where no one would immediately know her name.

At the time, Mel had read the stories and blamed the woman, like she was supposed to. Then they'd had a group discussion at school, about consent and date rape and listening when a person said no. and all the guys in class had laughed and the woman from social services giving the talk had flushed and sighed.

And that made Mel think.

But now, she knew.

§

"Leave the Miata here. I'll drive you over to the apartments." Ozzie stands in the garage office, feet planted and arms crossed, staring down that beautifully broken nose at Mel.

"That doesn't make sense." But it's tempting.

"Sure, it does. If the Miata stays here, that asshole won't figure out where you are."

"I thought you were getting your kids for the evening. Taking them out for pizza?"

"I am. I can drop you off at your Ma's place first, then pick you up and drop you at the farm after."

It's tempting. What would she do if Gunney showed up at the farm and she was out there alone? Hiding in the bathroom wouldn't work—no lock on the door to keep him out. Of course, she didn't have to let him in the house. All the house doors have locks.

But would he stay out?

"Okay." Mel agrees. She's feels like a coward, like someone running away. But she doesn't want to run. She wants to stay. She likes her job, her friends—even Delta. And she likes Ozzie—probably on her way to more than liking him.

She stares out at the Miata. What could she get for it in trade? She could buy something a little bigger, something the size of Ma's Impala, but newer. Something that Ozzie's legs fit in. Something that a could fit a couple of teenagers in the back seat.

"Don't let him run you off, okay?" Ozzie trails a finger down her cheek, bringing her back to the shop and him.

"I won't." Mel turns her face and smiles up at him, trying to make it reassuring and not weary.

He doesn't look like he believes her. "What happened with him over there?"

"Ozzie…" She sighs and closes her eyes. "It's complicated."

"I didn't think it would be simple. Shit never is."

Mel snickers and opens her eyes, staring up at Ozzie. His deep brown eyes bore into her soul, and she's surprised he can't tell. "We—well, actually, I guess I thought—we were in a relationship."

"*Thought* you were in a relationship?"

"It wasn't exclusive. I thought it was. I wanted it to be." Mel shrugs. "He was married and not working on the divorce like he kept saying. But I knew that. I lied to myself that he was."

Ozzie is quiet and Mel starts to worry. Has she just ruined anything that might have started?

"Lying is easy. I lied to myself about my marriage for a long time."

Mel peeks up at him. His face has grown serious, his eyes dark and intense.

"It felt real good when I stopped lying to myself. Once I faced the truth, things got better."

Better. Things were better now. Had she already faced the truth—at least part of it? The part about her Dad? That hadn't been lying, per se, but she hadn't understood the truth, and she did now, or at least more of it. She would never understand the whole of it, since he wasn't here to tell her. But she knew more than she had before.

"What if I don't know what the truth is?"

Sighing, Ozzie shifts and relaxes, leaning into one hip. "You can only know your own truth. I still don't know what Joanie is thinking or what she's going to do. But I've accepted she's being the best parent she can be, and I'm working on being the best one I can be, and I'm thankful my mother stepped in when she did."

Mel nods. "Put the kids first."

"That's part of it. I'm not letting folks spin me up and do stupid stuff anymore."

"Like hide in the bathroom?"

Ozzie snorts. "I never hid in the bathroom."

She tried to imagine Ozzie, all six foot plus of him, hunkered down in the little stall off the garage office and burst out laughing. "I suppose you didn't."

"Look, I'm not saying-"

"I know." Mel steps forward and wraps her arms around Ozzie, resting her cheek against his chest. He stiffens, and for a moment she's unsure. "I was the one hiding. But, no more. That's my plan, okay?"

He relaxes and wraps his own arms around her, slower and after a pause, drops a kiss on top of her head, leaving his lips pressed against the spot after.

"I wasn't expecting him to show up here. I'm not not sure what to say to him." She speaks into Ozzie's shirt.

"What do you want to say to him?"

She considers the question. What did she want to say? Go away. Leave me alone. Both of those are fine choices. But is there anything else?

No. There are things she'd like him to say to her. Admit that he'd assaulted her.

And there it is. The assault.

Mel stiffens.

Ozzie tightens his arms. "What?" He whispers into her hair, not letting her shift away.

Swallowing, she doesn't fight the embrace. "I got drunk over there. Lots of times. But, one time...Gunney...we...he...I didn't want to, but..." She can't make the words come out.

Squeezing her tighter, Ozzie rubs his cheek over her head. "Oh, Mel." His voice cracks.

He says nothing else. And that's okay. It wasn't her fault. She should have reported it. She's been told these truths more times than she can count. She doesn't need to hear them again.

"I'm sorry that happened to you."

His words sink in. He believes her. No question. No, *well you were drinking, weren't you? You'd had sex before, right?*

She'd been surprised when her mother had accepted her truth, but she'd needed her to accept it, to get mad about it. This was the same. It feels good, and another crack closes up.

Sighing, she sinks closer, squeezing her arms tighter.

And he squeezes her tighter, too.

§

"Your mother is, right. Leave the Miata at the garage." They walk together in the dark to his new car. "But I'm not sure you should be alone at the farm. He sounds smart enough to figure out where you live. It's not like it's a secret. So, I'll stay with you."

"Ozzie…" Mel starts the protest but lets it trail off. She's spent most of the evening fending off her mother's worries and fears. She can't fight her own. And a small part of her admits that she's unsure about staying alone. What if Gunney did show up? Leaving her car at the garage wasn't a guarantee that he wouldn't find out where she lived. "Fine."

"Fine?" Ozzie stops walking and stares down at her.

"Yes, fine." Mel speeds up, marching ahead, her prosthetic limp barely a hitch, toward Ozzie's ride. She knows her mother is watching from her window and doesn't want there to be too much for her to see.

"Just like that? Fine. I was expecting more arguing." Ozzie trots to catch up.

"So was I." Mel waits at the car, arms crossed, foot tapping. Maybe she shouldn't cave so easily. "But not this much. Not out of you."

Ozzie leans on the top of the car, palms slapping the surface. "So, why aren't you?"

Mel glares. "Because."

"So, we're going to argue over the lack of argument?" Ozzie straightens but leaves his arms stretched out.

"No," Mel points to the door, "we aren't going to argue. Let's get in the car before my mother comes out to find out why we haven't left yet."

Ozzie pressing the fancy remote unlock for his new car and all the door locks jump up.

Mel climbs in, the smell of unadulterated carpet and upholstery assaulting her nose. "You ought to deodorize this thing."

"Why? I thought the whole reason to deodorize a car was to make it smell new?" He slides the key in the ignition and the engine purrs, low and even.

Shrugging, Mel holds down the button for the passenger window and leans her elbow out. "Maybe it just needs to air out a bit."

Laughing, Ozzie shifts it into drive and they roll out of the parking lot.

"What about Lexie and Barry?" Guilt slides down her spine that she was taking Ozzie away from time with his kids.

"No worries. Mom called me while you were with your mother. Lexie asked about staying with a friend and after I said yes, Barry asked about having a friend over, and I let Mom answer yes to that, so...I'm taking them out for pizza tomorrow. Probably for put-put golf or bowling, too."

"Oh."

"You can come with us." Ozzie stares out the windshield.

Could she? "I've never played put-put."

Ozzie hisses. "Then we can go bowling."

"Your kids like bowling?"

He snickers and glances at her. "They like beating me at bowling."

"Ah. Will we play teams?"

"You and me against them?"

"Nah. I was thinking me and Lexie against you and Barry." Mel swings her head in his direction.

His bark of laughter startles her and she laughs in response, though she's not sure why.

"Lexie would probably like that." And his grin makes her feel easier about it.

"Warn her about my leg, okay?"

§

Mel is dozing when the sound of tires on gravel alerts her that they are nearing the farm. Blinking, she looks out into the dark. "We close?"

"Yeah, almost there."

"You didn't stop for a change of clothes?"

"Already got my bag in the back." He raises a hand when she jerks up in the seat. "It's always packed in case I get stuck at the fire house."

Settling back, Mel nods and runs her fingers through her hair. What is the matter with her, anyway? Why is she so jumpy? It's not like Ozzie plans to stay in her room. Right? She shoots him a side glance. Or is he?

"Ozzie...?"

"I'm taking the sofa, Mel." His soft laughter fills the car.

"Maybe I was going to ask you to sleep in my room."

The car jerks to a stop. She feels more than sees Ozzie staring at her. "Were you?"

"Well, no. But I might have been."

The car moves forward again, sedate, though Ozzie's breathing is harsh.

"Sorry." But Mel's voice is far from apologetic.

"S'okay."

"Ozzie?" Mel isn't sure she should ask.

"Yeah?"

"Do you want to sleep in my room?"

"No, Mel." Ozzie turns the car in a smooth arc onto the drive to the farm. "I don't want to sleep in your room."

"Oh."

"If I were in your room, with you, in your bed, we wouldn't be sleeping."

*Oh.* Mel slouches in her seat, silent, watching out the windshield for any of the cats.

"My turn to apologize?" Ozzie parks the car next to the refurbished truck and touches the button to pop the trunk.

"No. No reason to apologize." Mel steps out of the car and waits for Ozzie to fetch his bag. "I just..." She sighs.

Ozzie steps in front of her, the light from back step illuminating half his face, throwing the rest in sharp shadow.

"Sometimes, I want to not sleep with you." There. She's said it. Sort of.

Leaning down, Ozzie nudges her nose with his own. "Say it, Mel."

"I just did."

"No, no you didn't." He keeps his face close to hers.

"I want..." she swallows a lump in her throat, "I want to have sex with you."

"Just sex?" Ozzie leans down, his breath tickling her neck, followed by the warm caress of his lips on a spot above her collar bone.

"What else?"

He sighs. "Okay...sex."

"Ozzie?" Mel pushes him away enough to stare up at him.

His face is in shadows from the lamp at the back door, and she can't see his eyes. His eyes—if she could see them she'd know what he's feeling—she needs to see them.

She steps back and he remains where he was.

"I'm falling in love with you, Mel. I don't just want sex...I want..." It's his turn to swallow and he looks off to the dark tree line, "I want time with you, I want affection from you—and I want to give affection back to you—you know, holding hands or cuddling on the sofa. I want more."

Mel stares. Could she give all that to Ozzie?

She glances down at her hand and holds it out palm up.

He sets his hand in hers, his strong fingers twining through hers.

"I can't do that, all at once." Mel drags in a shaky breath. "I think I want it, I just...don't know if I'm a good person to give it to you." She closes her eyes. "I mean, the right person—I know I'm not a bad person."

"You're not the wrong person."

Mel looks at him; there is nothing but patience in his eyes, on his face.

"I can wait. I can't promise I won't want to rush or that I won't push for more...but-"

"Can we start with sex?" Mel steps towards him, reaching out with her other hand.

He takes it and grunts. "Sure." He sighs, the sound long and low and exaggerated. "We can start with sex."

Pulling her to him he nuzzles her temple. "But we're finding you a therapist, yeah?"

She nods. "Not with the VA, though."

He sets his lips to her neck. "Nope, not VA. I can ask my therapist for a recommendation. Someone in Richmond or Hampton?"

Mel sighs into his neck, fingers curling into his t-shirt. "Yeah. Sounds good."

Ozzie pulls back so he can see her eyes. "You mean that?"

Does she? Mel gazes into his eyes and find that she does. "Yeah. I want to. I want to know I can handle this, with you."

He smiles and closes his lips over hers, sucking once at her bottom lip. "Come on then."

# 21

## In the Bedroom

By the time they reach Mel's bedroom, Ozzie's shirt is off and his belt unbuckled, and Mel has her shirt unbuttoned and off her shoulders, letting it fall to the floor.

"Sweet Jesus." Ozzie reaches a hand to cup her breast, the heat of his palm buffered by the cotton of Mel's bra.

"More."

Her whispery plea does not go un-noticed, and Ozzie slips his hands around to her bra, making quick work of unclasping the fastener and tugging the fabric away.

"Ozzie?"

"Hmm?" He sounds like he's only half paying attention. His fingers traipse across her shoulders and down her chest.

"My leg."

"What about it?" His lips follow his fingers across one shoulder, while the fingers on her other side cup soft flesh, the thumb sliding over a tightening peak.

"I only have one."

Ozzie sighs and wraps his arms around her, rocking her from side to side. "If we're having sex, the pants have to come off."

"I know, it's...a warning." Mel sniffs. There is no way she's going to cry.

"I already know about your leg. I've seen it, remember?" Ozzie kisses her shoulder, then presses his lips to the space just above her collar bone.

"You haven't felt it."

Mel has. The skin is hardened and wrinkles and scarred and...and...

He hadn't smelled it, either; oh god, she had to take the sleeve off and it's been sweating all day.

"You want me to do that first. Now?" He pauses in his kisses.

She thinks. Does she? "Yes, but..." she sighs, "it's going to smell, too. It sweats in the sleeve."

He steps back, trailing a finger down her cheek. "Okay." Unbuttoning her trousers, he watches her face.

Mel looks down, focusing on his belly button. No lower—that area is off-limits for the moment.

The zipper slides down under the weight of his fingers, and he slips his hands inside to push the fabric down her legs. It catches at the hinge in the prosthetic, but he unhooks the denim and keeps pushing it down. He kisses the outside of her thigh. "Sit down."

She sits on the side of the bed, watching him.

He moves with care, methodical, shaking her trousers out before neatly folding them to drape over the back of the desk chair. When he turns back to face her, he has a soft smile on his lips.

Kneeling, he runs his hands down her thighs, making her shiver. When his hands reach her knees, he stops. "Mel?"

She swallows the lump in her throat, but still can't force any words to come out.

His fingers find the Velcro strap and pull it away, the rough rasp of the teeth pulling apart the only sound. Once the prosthetic is gone, his fingers return to her knee, the thumb caressing over the damp, damaged tissue.

Bending down, he keeps his eyes on her face, and Mel can't take her eyes away from him. Closing his eyes, he kisses the top of her thigh, letting his lips make their way to her knee when he stops. "Yeah, that's..."

Mel snickers. "You face."

"Let me get a washcloth." Ozzie stands and stalks to the bathroom in the hall, running the water to warm it up, when he returns, he has a soapy cloth in one hand and a towel in the other. Stooping, he carefully washes the stump then dries it.

Standing, he steps back into the hall and tosses the cloths toward the bathroom.

Watching him, Mel expects to feel embarrassed, but can't find a trace of the emotion anywhere.

Ozzie drops back to his knees in front of her, tracing his fingers over her thighs once more. "Where were we?" He bends his had back down, once again runnign his lips over her skin, stopping for little kisses and nips as he makes his way back down her leg.

When he reaches the scars, he doesn't stop.

Mel sobs and jerks her leg away.

"No, Mel. Shhh." Ozzie's voice is husky. "This is part of you now."

His lips and tongue drift over the reddened flesh.

Moaning, Mel closes her eyes and lets her head fall back. Her hands reach out to rest on Ozzie's shoulders.

She can feel the smile on his lips as they drift higher again, this time following a path up the inside of her thigh. "Lean back." He whispers against her flesh.

Mel sighs and complies, laying back on the bed, only her panties and one sock between her and Ozzie.

And then, her panties are gone, the single sock with it, and his lips brush against the lower part of her stomach. "May I?"

His hot breath sends a shudder through her womb and causes gooseflesh to erupt over her stomach.

"Yes."

He nuzzles against her mound and the shudders in her womb strengthen. Opening his mouth, he places kisses downward, his tongue darting into the moist area between her legs.

Mewling, Mel grips her bedspread, twisting, not trying to get away but to get closer.

His sigh causes more heat to form in her belly, the coil winding tighter. Cool palms press her thighs apart and his tongue dips in, swirling against the hard nub at the apex, then jabbing into her womanhood.

Mel pulses her pelvis up, back arching, neck pressing her head back into the mattress, gasping. Oh, it feels so good.

His tongue is replaced by fingers, long fingers, rubbing, sending little thrills through all her muscles.

The coil snaps and those muscles pulse and throb, waves of pleasure sweeping up and over Mel. She gasps, bucking against Ozzie's hand.

He presses his face to her stomach, fingers still inside her, his other hand stroking over her hip, down her thigh, to her scars. A kiss and a sweep of tongue, and Mel shudders again.

"Ozzie?"

"Hmm?"

"Get up here."

He snorts, the sound half laugh, and crawls up the bed.

"Wait." Mel holds up a hand and he freezes, worried eyes finding hers in the dim light.

She grins. "Take your jeans off first."

Complying, Ozzie pushes them down in a hurry, standing to stretch, watching her eyes take in the sight of him hard and full and ready, the tip off his manhood already glistening.

"Ready?" His voice is hoarse, and the rasp of it causes her to shiver.

"Fuck, yeah."

His eyes darken and he groans, stretching over her, pressing her into the mattress with his weight. The hair on his chest caresses her nipples and they harden.

Mel pulses up, cradling him between her thigh, her full leg hooking around him, her foot sliding between his legs.

Arching, she groans. "Please."

"Damn." Ozzie stiffens. "The condoms are in my bag."

"S'okay. I'm on the pill." Mel grinds up. "C'mon, Ozzie." She bites his shoulder.

"Don't rush me." Ozzie grins into her shoulder. "It's been a while since I've done this."

Mel glares at him through slitted lids. "Me, too."

Ozzie nuzzles his nose into her neck, stroking his tongue over her thumping pulse. "Truly?"

"No. Not since…" Mel winces; she'd almost forgotten about her leg, "not since Germany, at least."

"Germany?"

She sighs; her body is cooling. "The surgery."

Ozzie sucks on her neck, his fingers drifting over her chest, finding a breast to stroke, a nipple to pluck.

"M-hmm." He shifts his hips, his penis rubbing over her folds.

Mel warms again, the heat spreading, her blood thrumming once more. "Ozzie." Her wail is accompanied by an upward thrust, her good knee holding his hips in place. It almost works.

Ozzie chuckles and shifts again, his fingers sliding down her body to find her warm depths, holding her folds open. "Is this what you want?" He sets himself at her entrance, stroking himself only an inch inside.

"Gods, yes." Mel grinds out the words.

He thrusts in, filling her.

Mel arches, the feeling of him inside almost too much all at once, but at the same time just enough. She meets his downward thrust with an upward pulse of her own, meeting him, matching him, her muscles gripping him tight.

The coil builds again, the room filled only with their pants and grunts until Mel cries out as the sweeping waves of pleasure engulf her, and her whole body thrums with it.

Ozzie thrusts again, and again, harder, harder, then jams himself tight against her, pulsing, erupting in his own release.

# 22

## MORNING AFTER

Morning brings a hot, hard body pressed to Mel's back, a delicious awareness of her body, and an ache inside that still wants to be filled.

Sunlight drifts through the panes and window sheers, and Mel snaps fully awake.

The animals.

Groaning, she stretches and Ozzie's arms tighten around her; he moans into her neck. "Five more minutes."

"You can have five more minutes, I can't. Gotta take care of the animals."

Sitting up, Mel watches Ozzie's eyes flutter open and his gaze rise to meet hers. A smile spreads across his face, reaching his eyes, making them crinkle at the corners.

"Oh...good morning." His eyes leave hers to rove around this room. "Was this your room as a kid?"

Mel sighs and swings her leg over the side of the bed, reaching for the prosthetic lying on the floor. "Yeah."

"Nice."

She snorts but says nothing.

Ozzie sits up to, one hand stroking down her back. "You okay?"

Looking over her shoulder at him, Mel takes a moment to answer, then offers a soft smile. "Yes. I am. I'm better than okay."

Twisting around, she leans forward and kisses him.

Groaning he makes to wind his arms around her, but she stops him. "The animals."

He sighs. "Right, right. I'm getting up."

"You don't have to." Mel stands, a bit wobbly until she tightens the strap on her knee. It doesn't bother her.

"But I want to. This is part of your life now, right?" He stands and grabs his jeans, pulling them up his legs, not bothering with his briefs.

"Well, yes." Mel watches him, noting the way his muscles bunch and stretch with every move. He isn't cut, and would never make it as a magazine model, but he's fit and lean and she's flushed just looking at him.

"Hey," he walks towards her, "why do I have more clothes on than you?"

She snickers and smooths the Velcro on her prosthetic. "'cause you can go without undies."

Once dressed, they head downstairs, and Mel puts the coffee on to brew while they work. Grabbing jackets and boots and heading for the door, Ozzie pauses and grabs his keys from the counter where he'd dropped them the evening before. He dangles them in front of Mel. "I need to grab my bag."

Laughing, they make their way outside and to the barn.

Herbert is his usual aloof self, but the rest of the animals don't seem to mind Ozzie helping.

Closing the door, Mel grabs Ozzie's hand, squeezing it quick before dropping it. They could cuddle on the sofa after breakfast and watch a movie; maybe she could do this after all.

He leans down to kiss her, his lips lingering on hers. "I could get used to this."

At his car, Ozzie opens the trunk and pulls out his overnight duffle, snickering. "There's a while box of latex in there. If I'd known we wouldn't need it-"

The crackle of tires on gravel forces them to turn to the drive.

"Damn. He found me." It has to be Gunney. Who else would show up this early at the farm?

"Could be Brad."

"No, it couldn't." Mel waits, getting tenser the longer she waits for the car to edge around the corner of the house. When it does—a Mustang—she lets out a breath, the fear draining away.

"What?" Ozzie whispers.

"It's him. But you're here." Mel reaches out a hand to find his, wrapping her fingers around his.

Ozzie drops his bag to the ground and laces their fingers, pulling her closer.

Someone steps out of the Mustang and Gunney's voice rings out. "Mel?"

"Yeah. Over here."

Feet crunch gravel and Gunney steps into view. "Hey."

"Hey, yourself. What are you doing here?" Mel doesn't let go of Ozzie's hand.

"Looking for you." Gunney steps closer, a small smile spreading across his face.

"Why?" Mel wants him to leave.

"My divorce came through." He grins like it's the news she's been waiting for.

"Huh. Go figure. So did his." Mel tilts her head in Ozzie's direction.

Gunney stares. His gaze drops to their entwined hands. "I thought-"

"Well, I guess you thought wrong." It's Ozzie who speaks. When he laughs, low and steady, Gunney flushes red.

"Look, Gunney." Mel shifts but doesn't let go of Ozzie. She's not sure she could continue if she let go of him. "It's too late. Way too late. I'm in a better place now."

"A better place?" Gunney snorts. "You think he understands what happened to you?"

"You think you do?" Ozzie takes a menacing step forward.

For the first time Mel can remember, Gunney takes a step back from a threat. "What are you talking about?"

"I'm talking about what you did to her."

Should she stop him? Mel tightens her grip, and though Ozzie stops his forward momentum, he doesn't back down.

"I didn't do anything to her." Gunney spits out the words, and a jabbing finger points in her direction, but he doesn't look at Mel.

Mel flinches and jerks, like that finger made contact. His denial spurs an invasion of memories she doesn't want. The litany of *no, no, stop, no* that spilled from her lips. The hurt, the shame, the *come on, you want this*, followed by the gasping pants coming from the jerking body too heavy above her, teeth biting into her shoulder to keep her still. The struggle to get up, get out from under him, get her sleep shorts back up to her waist. To make his stop.

"Don't care what she told the punks at the VA." Gunney was no longer spitting, but he still wouldn't look at Mel.

So, he does remember. Is that why he's here? But what did he expect from her? Forgiveness? Understanding? Another toss in the sheets?

"It doesn't matter now." Mel is surprised at how strong her voice sounds. Inside, her stomach clenches, the muscles around it quivering. "I'm over it. So, you can leave."

"Leave?" Gunney finally looks at her, shock stretching over his features.

"Yes, Gunney. You can leave." Mel nods at his car. "Crawl back into your Mustang and go back to whoever you've been fucking since the divorce. Or before. Or find someone new to fuck. I don't care. Really, I don't."

Gunney stares a moment then turns and crawls back into the low-slung car. He guns the engine before spinning the tires in a tantrum of gears, and reverses, tearing up gravel and grass on his way back down the drive.

Mel sighs. "I don't think I'll get as much as I planned for the Miata."

"What?" Ozzie doesn't take his eyes off the red taillights disappearing down the road.

"Gunney. It's likely to be trashed before he leaves town."

"You think so?"

"I pretty much know so." Letting go of his hand, she stretches and smiles, hoping it's sultry and not tired.

Ozzie pulls out his phone and hits a recall button. "Hey, Trent? Can you swing by Gary's and make sure no one's messing with Mel's Miata?"

Mel watches him listen to whoever he's talking to. His face is in profile, the morning-peach light of dawn behind the sharp features.

"Yeah. Some guy was around asking about Mel earlier. That's why she left it at the garage. Didn't want him following her home."

He's gorgeous. Really. His Adam's apple bobs, and even that is sexy. She can't wait to get him inside. Maybe they could do more than just cuddle on the sofa.

"Thanks, Trent. Just be on the lookout." Ozzie punches another button and tucks the phone in his back jeans' pocket. He grins down at Mel. "That's that. I think your Miata will be fine."

"How?" Mel doesn't care. It's just a car. She glances at the old truck. If she trades them both in, she would have a hefty down payment on a new SUV.

"Mel?" He tips her chin to make her focus. "Trent's a cop. He's waiting for Gunney around the corner from the garage. If he tries anything, he'll be in jail for a week, at least."

Mel frowns. "That might make him angrier. Make him justify what he does."

Ozzie shrugs. "A police record might get him help. I think he needs it."

Leaning forward, Mel reaches up and cups his jaw, running her thumb over his bottom lip. "I know what I need."

"Yeah?" Ozzie leans close. "A therapist who will listen to you?"

She snickers, the laugh making her while body ripple. It would be nice to talk to someone about what happened with Gunney, someone who listened and didn't move the conversation on to the war stuff that happened. "Yeah, I need one of those. We can call your guy for a name later."

He smiles and brushes his nose against hers. "Someone to help you with the animals every morning and evening—unless there's a fire emergency?"

Mel shifts closer to him, wrapping her arms around him. "Yeah. Think Charlie's available?"

Ozzie jerks his head back to frown at her, and she laughs, throws her head back a little, feeling joys bubbling up.

"So you are aware," Ozzie glares at her, laughter dancing in his eyes, "Charlie hates, absolutely detests, animals."

"Ah." Mel winks. "I guess I'll have to settle for you then, huh?"

"Settle?" He palms her bottom with one hand, squeezing just a bit, enough to make her stomach swoop. "I'm great with animals. They love me."

They stare at each other, smiles gracing both of their faces.

Ozzie sighs and drops his lids to half mast. "Anything else you need?"

Mel straddles his thigh and undulates against it. "Yeah. And I can get more of it if we go inside and up to my room."

"Ah." Ozzie nods sagely, stepping back, and kisses her forehead. "Sleep. I'm sure you're tired. Busy night and all"

Mel doesn't say anything, but can't help the giggle that escapes, and simply takes his hand to lead him back into the house.

Ozzie's bag spends the day outside, too, forgotten and utterly unnecessary.

www.ingramcontent.com/pod-product-compliance
Lightning Source LLC
Chambersburg PA
CBHW061235210726

48293CB00003B/772